PASSION AND PONIES

(Chocoholics #2)

TARA SIVEC

Passion and Ponies
Copyright © 2014 Tara Sivec

Editing by Nikki Rushbrook and Donna Soluri.

Cover Art by Tara Sivec

Interior Design by Angela McLaurin, Fictional Formats
https://www.facebook.com/FictionalFormats

Also by Tara Sivec

Seduction and Snacks (Chocolate Lovers #1)
Futures and Frosting (Chocolate Lovers #2)
Troubles and Treats (Chocolate Lovers #3)
Hearts and Llamas (Chocolate Lovers Short Story)
Chocolate Lovers Special Edition
Love and Lists (Chocoholics #1)
A Beautiful Lie (Playing With Fire #1)
Because of You (Playing With Fire #2)
Worn Me Down (Playing With Fire #3)
Watch Over Me
Shame on You (Fool Me Once)

TABLE OF CONTENTS

Chapter 1 – Prancing Pony..1

Chapter 2 – A Happy Vagina is a Happy Life.............................8

Chapter 3 – Suck on Those Giblets..15

Chapter 4 – You are NOT the Father..23

Chapter 5 – Dick Nipples..32

Chapter 6 – Accidental Anal...39

Chapter 7 – Ass Captain...45

Chapter 8 – Pinky Pleasure or Butt Tower..............................53

Chapter 9 – Dolphin Rape..62

Chapter 10 – I Like Mushrooms...68

Amazon

Chapter 11 – I Will Not Have Sex With Tyler............................74

Chapter 12 – Hot and Juicy Wiener...................................82

Chapter 13 – Wood Chipper...88

Chapter 14 – Hoity Toity...94

Chapter 15 – Stripper Glitter..101

Chapter 16 – Pulsating Posey..107

Chapter 17 – Genital Flogging.......................................113

Chapter 18 – Sparkly Penis..119

Chapter 19 – Interstate..126

Chapter 20 – Fisting – For the Win..................................134

Chapter 21 – All the Feels...141

Chapter 22 – No Kink? No Problem..................................149

Chapter 23 – I Made a Poopy!..157

Chapter 24 – Merry Kiss My Ass.....................................165

Chapter 25 – Whinny Like a Horse..173

Chapter 26 – When You Wish Upon a Dildo.........................179

Chapter 27 – Friendship is Magic...187

Chapter 28 – BronyCon..195

Epilogue – Ava...204

Acknowledgements...209

For every Brony who's ever felt misunderstood.

CHAPTER 1

Prancing Pony

~ Ava ~

My eyes suddenly jerk open when I feel the subtle shaking of my bed. For a minute, my sleep-addled brain wonders if we're having an earthquake and panic sets in. Then I remember I live in Ohio and the house is probably not preparing to crumble down around me. As my eyes adjust to the darkness in my childhood bedroom, I listen intently for sounds of heavy breathing or the distinct metallic clang of a knife sharpening, certain the shaking of my bed is a not-so-stealthy axe murderer preparing to slit my throat.

What? That could totally happen. Some dude could have broken into my parent's home and now he's sitting on the edge of my bed, sharpening his giant knife.

I hold my breath in fear. I begin to slowly turn my head and prepare to come face-to-face with a homicidal maniac when

1

something kicks the back of my leg with the force of a two-by-four.

"Ouch! Son of a bitch!" I shout as I quickly flop over in bed. Unfortunately, I don't come face-to-face with a killer. What I do find in my bed next to me is much worse.

"Tyler! What the fuck are you still doing in my bed?" I whisper-yell, hoping my initial outburst didn't wake my parents, who are sleeping down the hall.

Tyler Branson, man-child extraordinaire and the guy I've been shame fucking for the past few months, doesn't even bat an eye at me. I listen in irritation as he lightly snores and watch as his legs jerk forward every couple of seconds. Pretty soon, his arms join in, reminding me of those stupid Youtube videos of dogs dreaming that they're running.

Almost immediately, a sound that can only be described as a *whinny* passes his lips as his arms and legs move at a faster pace, my bed bouncing with the force of his movements.

Oh, my God. Oh, sweet mother of Mary...

Reaching for my bedside table, I quickly turn on my lamp even though seeing Tyler swathed in any kind of lighting right now makes me want to puke. *This* is an image I don't want burned into my brain.

With my face scrunched up in disgust, I reach around his flailing arms and punch him in the chest. His eyes fly open in fear and he bolts up in bed, scrambling backwards until his back hits the headboard.

"What is it? What happened?" he asks frantically as he rubs the sleep from his eyes.

"What the hell were you doing?" I demand.

His eyes zone right in on my braless chest covered in a tank top. I quickly pull the sheet up to my chin and give him a dirty look.

"I was sleeping. What the hell did you wake me up for?" he complains.

"You kicked me and made a horse noise."

He stares at me blankly for a moment before scoffing at me in disbelief and sliding back down the bed until his head hits the pillow again.

"I was having a dream. Now leave me alone and let me go back to sleep."

When he rolls over, I shove my hand against his back. "Were you dreaming about horses? You were fucking *prancing* in your sleep."

Tyler looks over his shoulder at me and I watch his face redden with embarrassment. "What? You're delusional. I don't prance. I NEVER prance."

I just shake my head at him. "You were totally prancing in your sleep. Prancing and *whinnying* like a damn horse."

"You shut your face! Shut your face right now!" he shouts.

I shove my finger close to his nose. "No, YOU shut your prancing face, Twilight Sparkle, before my parents hear you. You're not even supposed to BE here. You were supposed to sneak out of my bedroom window just like always. Get out of my bed!"

He huffs in irritation and angrily flings the blankets off of him before getting out of bed. My already black soul dies a little more inside when I can't tear my eyes away from his perfect ass and his chiseled abs as he pulls his clothes on, muttering under his breath the entire time.

This was never supposed to happen. Sleeping with Tyler was supposed to be a one-time thing – a means of scratching an itch and quelling the boredom that has consumed my life lately. The first time we had sex and he sang the theme song from My Little Pony while he went down on me should have sent me running for the hills like my ass was on fire. He's immature, he constantly pisses me off and he's twenty-five years old and can't hold down a job to save his life.

But dammit, sex with Tyler was the biggest high I've ever had in my life.

It's official: I am clinically insane.

I am twenty-one-years old and I hate my life. Okay, maybe hate is a strong word. I'm *dissatisfied*. I took a leave of absence from college because wasting my parents' money when I had no idea what I wanted to do with my life was pointless. I've been working at my mother's company, Seduction and Snacks, as an administrative assistant for the past few months and hating every minute of it. My mother co-owns the business with her best friend Claire. Mom's side is the Seduction half of the equation. They sell all things sex from toys, porn and games to lingerie and costumes. Claire operates the Snacks side, where they make the best damn baked goods ever to hit the Midwest. Sounds amazing, right? I should love the fact that my family has made a small fortune over the years and that Seduction and Snacks is now located in twenty-eight states throughout the U.S. I should also enjoy working in the family business and take pride in the fact that my mother and my Aunt Claire started building this empire when they were only a few years older than me.

Maybe that's my problem. They were my age when they came up with this idea and they made it a reality only three years later. I don't have any earth shattering, groundbreaking ideas. I have nothing that's just mine alone, except a fashion blog where I talk about clothes and purses and other things that interest me. I'm expected to work at Seduction and Snacks and continue living *their* dream. It's not my dream, though. I have no fucking clue what my dream is aside from finding a good sale at Nordstrom's for those Michael Kors wedge pumps I've had my eye on.

Which brings us back to Tyler. And no, *he's* not my fucking dream either! He's just a way to keep my mind off of the fact that I'm in my early twenties and clueless about where my life is going. Obviously, it's going nowhere fast with Tyler and I need to nip this thing in the bud immediately.

Tyler pulls his shirt down over his head and I pretend like I'm not sad to see his naked abs go.

"I can't believe you're kicking me out at three-o'clock in the morning," he grumbles as he slides his feet into tennis shoes without bothering to tie them.

He walks over to my window and slides it open, looking back at me and smirking. "So, same time, same place tomorrow?"

Rolling my eyes, I shake my head. "No. Absolutely not. We're not doing this anymore. Leave and don't come back."

He's got one leg swung over the windowsill and his body

halfway out before he jerks his head back inside and stares at me in surprise. "What? What do you mean 'don't come back'? Like, don't come back tomorrow, or ever?"

Seriously, how can he be so dense?

"Ever. This was a huge mistake."

He actually has the nerve to growl at me. Thank God he didn't whinny or I'd be puking right into my lap.

"Fine! But you'll be begging for another piece of Tyler, mark my words!"

"Jesus Christ, don't talk about yourself in third person," I complain.

"They come back, they always come back to Tyler," he mutters with another smirk, completely ignoring me.

"By 'they', I'm assuming you're talking about the ponies you were dreaming about?" I chuckle.

"Fuck your face! Fuck your face right now!" he demands.

"Get the hell out of my bedroom and don't come back, Prancer!" I fire back.

Sticking his tongue out at me in one poorly-executed, last ditch effort to put me in my place, he tries to smoothly exit my window but his head smacks against the frame. He lets go of the sill to grab his wounded head and loses his balance, falling out the window and into the shrubs on the other side.

"Mother fucking dick fuck ass cake piece of shit shrub!" I hear him whisper from the yard.

Getting out of bed, I rush over to the window, slam it closed and secure the lock. I climb back into bed, turn off my light and try to think about anything other than Tyler Branson and his stupid tongue.

I can totally quit Broke Back Moron, piece of cake.

CHAPTER 2

A Happy Vagina is a Happy Life

- Tyler -

"My life is over," I wail, plopping myself down in the chair across from Gavin's desk.

He looks up from his computer and cocks his head. "So you got fired from The Gap? You didn't like that job anyway."

I stare at him in confusion and shake my head sadly. "I'm sorry, have we met? Who gives a shit about The Gap? I'm talking about Ava. I'm pretty sure she's not going to have sex with me anymore."

In all honesty, I am kind of pissed about getting fired. It's not like working at The Gap was a dream job, but it paid for porn and strip clubs so it had some perks. I gave those assholes two of the best months of my life and what do they do? Get audited by corporate and tell me the copy of my birth certificate I gave them when they hired me was a fake. As if!

"I thought you couldn't stand Ava?" Gavin asks in confusion.

"I can't. All she does is bitch at me. But man alive, that chick's got a mouth like a Shop Vac."

Gavin winces and mimics dry heaving. "Seriously dude, stop. Just stop."

Gavin and I have been best friends ever since we met our freshman year in college. It's unfortunate that I was naked during that first meeting, but what can you do? Sometimes the boys just like to dangle while you're hanging pictures around your dorm room. Anyway, as soon as we got to talking (after I put pants on), I knew this was a guy I wanted in my corner. He's a good-looking dude, so he's always had a plethora of hot chicks sniffing around him. Lucky for me, he's been in love with Charlotte, his childhood sweetheart, since birth and I, therefore got all his castoffs.

Some dudes would probably be offended at being the second-best choice. Those dudes are obviously dumb fucks who don't know rule number one in the guy handbook - you never, ever turn down pussy. Gavin's feelings towards Charlotte are obviously not brotherly, but he's always looked at Ava as a little sister. Needless to say, talk about our sexcapades grosses him the fuck out.

"I guess I shouldn't let it get to me. I mean, how can I bang a chick that has no appreciation for animals?" I ask in irritation as I kick my feet up on his desk.

"I'm pretty sure Ava loves animals. I think the problem is that she didn't expect to sleep with one," Gavin replies with a smirk.

I knew I shouldn't have told him about that whole horse incident the other night.

"So what's on the agenda today, dick licker? Are we going to watch some chicks masturbate, maybe construct a mold of my penis for a new sex toy?" I ask, quickly moving the conversation away from my embarrassing evening with Ava.

Gavin has worked in Product Development for Seduction and Snacks ever since graduating from college. Lucky bastard.

Shaking his head at me, he gets up from behind the desk and heads towards the door. "How many times do I have to tell you that no one masturbates inside this building?"

"And how many times do I have to tell you that I don't like it when you lie to me and crush my dreams," I remind him as I follow him out into the hall.

Luckily, Ava isn't at her desk right outside Gavin's office. She works part time as his secretary and I made sure to stop by today when she was on her lunch break. Actually, regardless of what time I stop by, chances of her ass being in that desk were miniscule. That chick is hot as fuck and the best lay I've ever had, but working is not her strong suit.

"Our tour guide for the warehouse was in a pretty bad car accident over the weekend, so I'm stuck taking over the tours until we can find a replacement," Gavin explains as he pushes open the double doors to the warehouse.

I've strolled through the warehouse and even participated in a few tours, but each time I walk through those doors is like the first time. I swear as soon as I set foot in this place I can hear a choir of angels singing. As far as the eye can see, row after row, aisle after aisle, box after box – are sex toys. Metal shelving from floor to ceiling filled with boxes of beautifully crafted love machines.

I don't even realize I'm mumbling until Gavin punches me in the arm.

"Were you just chanting 'This is my home; this is where I belong'?"

I just shrug and follow him over to the first aisle, where a group of about ten women ranging in ages from twenty-five to sixty-five stand, anxiously awaiting their tour of Mecca.

"No talking, no crying, no sword fights with the dildos and please, for the love of God, do NOT lick the Chocolate Thunders on aisle twelve again," Gavin warns me under his breath.

Is it my fault they named a sex toy after chocolate? How the fuck was I supposed to know it didn't taste like chocolate? That's false advertising, if you ask me.

"Ladies, welcome to Seduction and Snacks! My name is Gavin and I'm the head of Product Development. If you'll just follow me, we can start the tour."

"This one has slow pulses along with intense vibrations. It's got an easy two-button functionality and you'll be happy to know it's made from durable, phthalate-free plastic. I would highly recommend this toy for any of you first-timers who just aren't sure how to start when building your toy collection. It's one of our most popular models and I guarantee you'll enjoy it."

Gavin was called away from the tour a half hour ago for an emergency conference call. I felt bad for all these bitches standing around waiting for him, so I figured I might as well carry on with the tour.

Placing the toy back into its bin on the shelf on aisle fourteen, I look up from the crowd of women surrounding me and see Gavin and his Aunt Liz standing at the edge of the group. Gavin is smiling and Liz has a look of complete shock on her face.

I excuse myself from the group, leaving them to chat amongst themselves as I make my way to Gavin and Liz.

"What the fuck was that?" Liz asks as soon as I reach her.

Awwww shit, now I'm in trouble. I should have just wandered over to the flavored lube on aisle seven and had a snack. The funnel cake flavored lube really is quite filling.

"That was the Eighth Wonder of the World. You know, one of the toys you sell here?" I remind her.

I barely finish my sentence when her hand flies out and smacks me up side the head. "I'm well aware of toy's name, dick face. I meant, how did *you* know so much about it? You sounded like you could have written the fucking product description for it."

Oh, is that all?

"Well, I'm kind of a connoisseur of sex toys, if you will. I like to keep myself informed for the ladies. A happy vagina is a happy life," I tell her with a smile.

"Eeew, that's disgusting," Liz complains. "I can't believe I was actually thinking about giving you a job."

Gavin's face lights up and he turns to face her. "Seriously?

Aunt Liz, that would be awesome! Finally, something better than that stupid clothing store."

I gasp, placing my hand over my heart. "That hurts, Gavin, that really hurts. Have you ever taken off all of your clothes and curled up in a box of cotton blend t-shirts? It's like floating on a cloud."

"Forget I said anything," Liz mutters, turning to walk away from us.

Gavin grabs her arm, forcing her to stop. "Wait, Aunt Liz, just hear me out. Tyler might be an idiot, but he really does know a shit ton about our products. He could recite the specifications for everything we carry in his sleep."

Liz raises an eyebrow and looks at me.

"It's true. I've been known to talk about twirling beads, rotating shafts and cock rings during a night of peaceful slumber," I admit.

"Oh my God, this is the worst idea in the history of the world. I must be high," Liz mutters.

"Hey, what a coincidence, so am I!" I tell her with a smile.

Gavin punches me in the arm and I scowl at him.

"I cannot believe I'm actually considering this," Liz sighs. "Here's the deal. I just found out that our guy who usually gives the tours won't be coming back. He hurt his knee pretty bad in the accident and he's not going to be able to stand for the long periods of time that tours require. Right now, I just need someone to fill in until we make a more permanent decision. You have to be friendly, informative and you absolutely CANNOT have sex with anyone on the tour."

"Fuck it, I'm out," I complain.

That earns me another smack from Gavin. Seriously, does he really expect me to work in a sex toy warehouse, playing with toys all day long and not have sex with anyone? I wonder if that includes myself. It better not include myself, that's just wrong.

"He'll take the job," Gavin answers for me.

And just like that, I'm a working man again.

CHAPTER 3
Suck on Those Giblets
~ Ava ~

"YOU DID WHAT?!"

I realize my voice might be a little high when my mother winces and covers her ears. But seriously, she must be joking.

"Please tell me you did NOT hire Tyler to work at Seduction and Snacks. Are you insane?" I ask, abandoning the email on my iPhone announcing a seventy-percent off sale on Coach purses that I should be writing a blog post about right now. Only something this insane could tear my eyes away from the new coral colored Peyton leather satchel.

It's so pretty I want to pet it.

"According to the doctors, no, I am not insane. Borderline, with homicidal tendencies towards my children, but that's understandable," she replies with a smile.

Before I completely lose it and start throwing a hissy fit, I should probably warn you that my mom, Liz, is not like other moms. She says whatever she thinks and has no filter. We have an unconventional relationship in that she doesn't hesitate to call my sisters or me assholes and my sisters and I are content to continue acting like assholes just to get her riled up. Sometimes it's fun to watch my mom lose her shit. She's obviously determined to turn the tables today.

It's no secret that my mother doesn't really like Tyler, which makes it even more alarming that she actually hired him to work for her company. *I* don't even like Tyler. I'm still trying to figure out why in the hell I ever slept with him in the first place. And then repeated that mistake. Eighteen times.

"You have to fire him. Immediately. Tell him you made a mistake or something," I beg.

There is no way I can go to work at that place every day knowing he's going to be there. It's bad enough he shows up unannounced all the time to hang out with Gavin; this would be much worse and make me hate that job more than I already do.

My mom rolls her eyes and takes a seat at the kitchen table. "If you're going to continue sleeping with him, he needs a better job than folding sweaters at the mall."

"I am NOT sleeping with him!" I argue, stomping my foot and putting my hands on my hips.

Technically, I'm not lying. I'm not sleeping with him right this second.

"Oh, please. I heard barnyard animal noises coming from your room the other night and someone shouting 'Pull my reins, bitch!' I realize you're twenty-one-years old and theoretically an adult, but if I have to hear that shit one more time when I'm trying to sleep, I will beat you like a red-headed step child," she warns.

Did I also mention my mom is sort of the coolest mom ever and has never threatened my life the many times she's caught me having sex? She's always been of the opinion that telling us not to do something will just make us want to do it even more. As soon as my sisters and I got our periods, she marched us down to the doctor, put us on the pill and gave us a lifetime supply of condoms.

Still, knowing she heard Tyler and I having sex makes me feel dirty.

"That must have been a movie I was watching in my room. I'll make sure to keep the volume down from now on," I tell her, attempting to lie.

She scoffs and rolls her eyes at me. "Really? A movie? So you've taken up watching horse porn now, have you? Actually, I think I'd rather you were watching horse porn than sleeping with Tyler."

I ignore her and walk over to the counter to pour myself a cup of coffee.

"Mom, you can't be serious about hiring Tyler to work at Seduction and Snacks. He never shows up for work on time and he's got no work ethic," I complain.

"And yet, I hired you, didn't I?" she asks with a laugh.

"Oh, you're hilarious."

She's right, but it still sucks to hear it. How can I possibly show up on time and be expected to work when I don't care about what

I'm doing? Shouldn't you be passionate about your career? The only thing I'm passionate about is spending my paycheck on a new Coach purse.

Just then I hear the front door open and a shout from my sister, Charlotte. "Hello? Is anyone home?"

"We're in the kitchen," mom yells back.

Charlotte walks in the room and gives mom a kiss on the cheek before walking up to me and taking the coffee cup out of my hand. "What's up, skank?"

"Nothing much, twat. I spit in that coffee, by the way," I inform her as she takes a sip.

"So that's why it tastes like rotten vagina," she tells me with a smirk.

"There's so much love in this room I almost can't stand it," mom adds, standing up from the table. "I have to run some errands. Play nice, you two. No fighting, no biting and no hair pulling. I still have bruises from the last time you two were alone in the same room together."

I love my sister, but we have a tendency to butt heads a lot. We always make up right away and never hold grudges against one another, but we've been known to break a few pieces of furniture and one of us usually ends up bleeding. My mom says we've been that way since we were old enough to walk. Our very first fight happened when Charlotte was five and I was two. Charlotte handed me a cupcake she'd made out of Play-Doh and told me to eat it. Being two, I did it without question and promptly puked up the Play-Doh cupcake all down the front of my favorite princess costume. I walked right up to Charlotte and kicked her in the cooch wearing my tiny, black patent leather Mary Janes. I'd seen my Uncle Carter do it to my Uncle Drew and it seemed like it hurt pretty bad, so I figured it would work on Charlotte. My mom said she thought two cats were eating each other's faces off by the sounds of the screams coming from our bedroom.

"So what's new with you? Still sleeping with Tyler the Turkey?" Charlotte asks with a laugh.

I made the mistake of telling Charlotte a little secret about something Tyler does whenever I'm giving him a blow job. Tyler is a talker in bed, and when I'm going down on him, it's even worse. He likes to coordinate said talking with whatever holiday is closest. The blow job in question was right before Thanksgiving. Tyler really got into the spirit of things, gobbling like a turkey while I had his dick in my mouth and yelling out "Yeah, baby! Suck on those giblets."

Do you see now why I kicked him out of my bed the other night? How can I possibly continue to sleep with someone who refers to his balls as turkey organs?

"I thought we agreed to never speak of that again? And no, I'm not sleeping with him anymore. I gave him the boot and told him to never come back," I tell her, pouring myself another cup of coffee.

"Didn't you tell him you would never sleep with him again after he told you to lick his little pumpkins on Halloween?" Charlotte laughs.

"Fuck off," I mutter. "Change of subject. How's married life?"

Charlotte rolls her eyes. "Shut up. We're not married."

"You're living in sin and finish each other's sentences – close enough. It's cute and disgusting all at the same time. He's probably going to propose on Christmas."

Her eyes widen and her mouth drops open. "Oh, my God. Do you think he will? No, there's no way! It's too soon! We've only been living together for a few months. Holy shit, what if he does? What should I wear?"

It's my turn to roll my eyes. She's so giddy and in love that it makes me want to punch her in the throat. I'm happy for her and Gavin, I really am. They have been friends since birth due to the fact that our parents are best friends and we all grew up together. A few months ago, they each decided it was time to admit their true feelings about one another. They both went about it the wrong way, making a list of ways to prove their love to each other instead of just coming right out and saying it. Charlotte's gay best friend pretended to be her boyfriend and Gavin pretended he was dating some bat shit crazy ex-girlfriend of his who wound up beating the shit out of a dude in the bar one night and calling him a Vaginaman. It was a hot mess, but it all ended well. They've been shacking up for the last few months and they work at Seduction and Snacks together. It's so perfect I want to gouge my eyes with a fork.

I'm woman enough to admit that I'm a little bit jealous. My only prospect for love is a man who lights his farts on fire and has a membership to a porn-of-the-month club. I really need to get back into the dating world and forget about Tyler once and for all.

"I'll take you shopping for the perfect proposal outfit, and I'll even buy it for you if you help me find a man," I tell her.

Even though Charlotte and I fight a lot, we still have one thing in common – our love of shopping. Her eyes light up at the idea of going to the mall and she holds out her hand.

I grab onto it and we shake, making a deal.

"Done. I have the perfect guy in mind for you. Don't make any plans for tomorrow night. Do you have something slutty to wear?"

She looks me up and down, focusing on the tight, low-cut shirt I'm wearing that barely contains my boobs and the short, pleated skirt that stops right below my ass that I paired with black, knee-high stiletto boots.

"Never mind. I see you've already been shopping at Sluts R Us."

She leaves me no choice but to wrap my arm around her neck and put her in a choke hold.

"Goddammit, cut it out, asshole!" she yells at me as I bend over, taking her down with me.

She begins smacking my legs and I start pulling her hair, both of us screaming and cursing.

"STOP BEING SUCH A BITCH! I CAN'T BELIVE YOU- hey, is this the new Mossimo Pointe Stripe jacket?" I ask, pausing to pull the tag out of the neck of Charlotte's coat.

"Yes! I got it on sale at Target. Isn't it cute?" she asks, her head still down by my waist as I read the tag.

"You should have paired it with some skinny Seven jeans and those black Steve Madden pumps you wore to the DMV in August," I tell her, finally releasing my stranglehold so she can stand.

She smoothes down her hair that was mussed during our tussle and stares at me like I'm crazy. "How is it that you can precisely recall what I wore three months ago but you can't remember how to use the photocopier at work?"

I shrug, turning away from her to grab my keys off of the counter. "It's not that I'm incapable of remembering how that machine works, I just choose NOT to remember. It's boring."

"What was I wearing when we went to the Pink concert?" she asks.

"September 23rd? You had on a black Max and Mia drawstring waist dress with nude, Valentino couture bow platform pumps," I reply as I head out of the kitchen and towards the front door.

"October 15th?" she asks, following me outside towards my car.

"J Brand skinny stretch jeans, black Stuart Weitzman knee boots and a fitted, emerald green Donna Karan ¾ length t-shirt," I rattle off easily as I unlock my doors.

Charlotte stands next to the passenger side door, staring over the top of the car at me in awe. "Jesus Christ, you're like the Rain Man of fashion. Why the hell are you working at Seduction and Snacks? You should be taking over Nordstrom's."

I roll my eyes and laugh as we both get into the car.

"Believe me, if I could find a way to make money talking about clothes, shoes and purses, I would be all over that shit."

As we head towards the mall, I try not to think about Tyler or how much I hate my job. Charlotte is going to set me up with a new guy and maybe my life will finally start looking up.

Dating world, here I come.

CHAPTER 4

You are NOT the Father

- Tyler -

"I'd like to thank the Academy for this illustrious award," I speak into the mirror in my room, straightening my imaginary tie. "I'm humbled that so many of my peers thought I was deserving of the Dapper Dildo Award."

Do they give out awards at Seduction and Snacks? Eh, if they don't now, I'm sure they will after I've been in their employ for a few weeks.

I can't contain my excitement as I think about the fact that I have a real job. A real, honest to God job that I can be proud of and brag to people about on the street. I mean, The Gap was a pretty good gig - all the sweater vests I could handle and plenty of hot pieces of ass hitting on me every day. They were all gay dudes, but whatev. They appreciated a good thing when they saw it.

I've been trying to get my foot in the door at Seduction and

Snacks ever since I found out Gavin's family owned the business. I make sure to keep myself current on all things sex. I've committed to memory the name, cup size and favorite sexual position of every female porn star of the last decade. I'm an expert on all things fetish, from sacofricosis and ederacinism to mucophilia and oculolinctus. I've even volunteered on more than one occasion to be a human guinea pig for new Seduction and Snacks products. I have the organic plaster they were tinkering with for penis molds to thank for the fact that I couldn't grow hair on my balls for three months. A few months of shiny, smooth balls were well worth the third degree burns I sustained on my taint when I tried to use a hair dryer to remove the plaster, especially if sacrificing a few pubes led to Liz realizing my full potential.

Maybe now that I have a good job, Ava will stop being such a bitch and sleep with me again. Grabbing my cell phone off of my dresser, I decide to shoot her a text and deliver the good news.

Hey there, loose labia. Wanna carpool in to work tomorrow? I'll let you give me a blow job in the parking lot.

Satisfied that my news will thaw a little of the ice in her veins, I toss my phone back on my dresser and head upstairs to look for a good copy of my birth certificate.

Yes, I live in the basement of my parents' home. I get twenty-eight cable channels, access to all the porn my dad still has on VHS and meatloaf every Thursday night. Seriously, why would I leave?

Opening the door at the top of the stairs that leads into the kitchen, I stop in my tracks when I see my dad sitting up on the counter with his feet in the sink and my mom standing next to him shaving his legs.

"Oh, hi, sweetie! Do you need the sink?" my mom asks, smiling brightly as she squirts some extra shaving cream on my dad's shin.

Alright, maybe there's at least one reason to move out and get my own place.

"Mom, seriously? I just ate lunch. Do you want me to puke all over the floor?" I ask disgustedly as I avoid looking directly at them.

"Tyler, studies have shown that a man and a woman who share simple, every day experiences like this will have a long and fruitful sex life," my dad says, looking up from what my mom's doing and pushing his glasses up higher on his face.

"I shaved your father's balls for the first time when we were twenty-one and look at us now! We're still going strong twenty-six years later and our love making is more passionate than ever," my mom tells me with a smile.

Shaking my head at them, I keep my eyes averted as I head over to the built-in desk on the other side of the kitchen.

"I like the feel of smooth legs. I totally get why women have been doing this for centuries," my dad adds.

Really, their behavior shouldn't come as any surprise to me at this point. My parents, Donna and Nick Branson, are sex therapists. There was a time when I attributed my love of sex to their constant discussion of the topic, but now I worry all this "sharing" is going to one day seriously effect my ability to keep it up. Last week when

I got home from work, I found them in the living room practicing their climax yells. Fully clothed, sitting on the couch, legs crossed like they were attending church services, screaming each other's names in different pitches to see which one sounded the best.

Ignoring my parents' giggles on the other side of the room, I dig through the desk drawers, tossing papers aside as I go. I grow more and more frustrated as I open drawer after drawer, and my parents' laughter gets more and more intimate. I know if I don't find what I'm looking for and get the fuck out of here, vegetables from the fridge will soon be added to the mix - and they won't be used for tonight's salad.

Where the fuck is it? I swear there was a copy in here.

"Sweetie, what are you looking for?"

Glancing up from the mess I've made on the top of the desk, I sigh, slamming the drawer closed. "I need something for my new job."

"Oh, no! Did you get fired from The Gap? Were you trying on all the clothes naked again? I told you they were going to be angry about that."

Geez, you have one runway show after hours and everyone loses their shit.

It's not my fault I didn't realize they had security cameras in the storage room. And really, they should have used that footage for a commercial. I worked the SHIT out of those boxer briefs and scarves.

"No, this time it wasn't my fault. They claim my birth certificate is a fake. Can you believe that? As if," I complain with a roll of my eyes. "I got hired at Seduction and Snacks. I start tomorrow and need to take a non-fake copy in."

My mom and dad look at each other nervously, sharing some silent communication shit before my dad hefts himself out of the sink.

"I think it's time, Donna," my dad tells her, grabbing a towel from the counter and wiping the shaving cream off of his legs.

"You're right. It's time for me to make dinner. Who wants meatloaf?" she asks with fake enthusiasm.

My dad grabs her arm before she can make it to the fridge, turning her to face him. I watch in confusion as he whispers a few words to her before they both turn to face me.

"Tyler, I think you should sit down," my dad begins.

"Dude, this isn't the end of the world," Gavin tells me as I continue splashing cold water on my face in his bathroom.

I showed up at his and Charlotte's apartment twenty minutes ago and have been in the bathroom the entire time trying to calm the fuck down.

"Not the end of the world? NOT THE END OF THE WORLD? I don't know who I am! I don't know where I came from. I'VE LOST MY IDENTITY!" I scream, shutting off the water and reaching blindly for a towel.

My hand brushes up against one and I quickly bring it to my face, wiping off the water that drips down my lips and chin.

"Oh shit, I wouldn't use that towel if I were you," Gavin mumbles.

I ignore him, scrubbing every inch of my face, hoping that maybe I can rub away the memory of the words my mother spoke to me.

"Tyler, your father isn't really your father. I, um… I don't actually know who your real dad is," my mom admitted. "I really wanted a baby and I wasn't seeing anyone at the time, so I went to a sperm bank. Also, when I say I wasn't seeing anyone, I mean I wasn't serious with anyone. I was still having lots of sex."

"Son, what your mother is trying to say is that she was sexually adventurous in her twenties," my dad added with a smile.

"If we're going to be honest with him, we might as well do it right," my mom cut in. "Tyler, I was a slut. Like, a really big one. I was young, though, and that's what you're supposed to do — sow your wild oats. I also went through a short lesbian phase, but that's beside the point."

I sank down into one of the chairs at the kitchen tabled and stared at them. "How in the hell did this happen?"

"Well, I picked out the sperm I wanted and then the doctor had me get on the table with my feet in the stirrups. Then he took a thing that looked like a turkey baster and shoved it up my-"

"NO! JESUS CHRIST, NO! Not that part! How the hell don't you know who my father is if you used a sperm bank? Don't they keep a record of that shit?" I asked in confusion.

"Well, normally that would be helpful, but I also had a foursome that same week. I'm pretty sure one of them was a woman I met in the food court of

the mall, but the other two guys – no clue. I always made my partners bag it up, but something must have leaked because I found a little jizz in my-"

"MOM!" I screamed at her, shaking my head in disgust.

"Sorry, sweetie. Since sperm can live in a woman's vagina for up to five days, I can't be certain if it was donor sperm or…" my mom trailed off before glancing over at my dad with love in her eyes.

"Anyway, I met your father when you were a couple of months old and he adopted you. Sort of. We actually never filed the paperwork, but we made a very convincing copy of a birth certificate for you in Photoshop."

My dad walks over to me and pats me on the back. "I think the best thing for us to do right now would be to sit down and talk about what we're feeling. I'll start. I'm feeling relieved that this is all finally out in the open."

"I'm feeling like I want to puke all over this fucking floor!" I shouted.

My mom walked over to me and put her arm around my shoulder. "That's it. Let it all out, sweetie."

"Seriously dude, give me that thing," Gavin says, interrupting my thoughts.

I pull the towel away and glare at his reflection in the mirror. He's standing behind me with a look of disgust on his face and his hand out.

"What the fuck is wrong with you? I just found out that my mom was a slut and has no idea who my dad is and all you're worried about is your precious towel?" I ramble, my voice getting that hysterical squeak to it. "What's wrong? Is this one of Charlotte's 'good' towels, reserved for guests or some shit? Fuck, are you pussy whipped."

Gavin shakes his head at me and tries reaching over my shoulder to take the towel. I snatch it away and turn to face him.

"What is your fucking deal? It's a Goddamn towel!" I yell.

"Yeah, it's a jizz towel, dude."

I look at him in confusion, glancing down at the towel and back up at him when what he said finally sinks in. He's biting his lip and I can't tell if he's trying not to laugh or if he's trying to think of a way to run out of here as fast as he can.

"Hey, what are you guys doing in the bathroom?" Charlotte asks, suddenly appearing in the doorway. "Oh, my God! Did you just use that towel, Tyler?"

I quickly throw the towel away from me like it's on fire and it lands in the toilet.

"Dammit, don't throw it in the toilet, you'll ruin it!" Charlotte scolds.

"I'm pretty sure you ruined it by putting jizz on it!" I scream. "Why the fuck would you leave a jizz towel on the sink where anyone could use it?"

Charlotte shoulders past us and uses the tips of her fingers to pull the towel out of the toilet and then tosses it into the sink.

"I'd never use it. I knew it was a jizz towel," Gavin replies with a shrug.

"Oh, my God! I scrubbed my fucking face with a towel that had your dry, crusty jizz on it!"

I can't believe this is happening right now. My mom had a foursome, my dad isn't my dad and now I have jizz face. Moving as fast as I can, I jump into the shower and turn on the water, not even caring that I'm fully clothed.

"Do you want us to leave so you can take your clothes off?" Charlotte asks, as the water rains down on me, soaking my t-shirt and jeans.

"I am NOT taking my clothes off. There could be trace particles of jizz on them! I'm going to have to burn these clothes!" I complain.

I keep my face under the scalding hot water, taking in large mouthfuls, swishing and then spitting on the shower floor.

"Eeeew, don't spit in our shower!" Charlotte scolds.

"I HAVE GAVIN'S JIZZ ON MY FACE! I WILL SPIT WHEREVER THE FUCK I WANT!"

Gavin grabs Charlotte's arm and pulls her towards the door. "How about we just give you a few minutes alone? We'll be out in the living room. There are *clean* towels under the sink."

I give him a dirty look when he mentions towels.

"Any and all jizz that was previously on those towels has been washed off, I swear," Gavin adds before exiting the room and closing the door behind him.

With a sigh, I stand under the water until it starts to get cold.

CHAPTER 5

Dick Nipples

~ Ava ~

"I can't believe you're making me do this. I don't want to see him," I complain, flopping down on the couch.

"Stop being a bitch to him for two seconds. Tyler is having a really bad day and he could really use some support."

I bristle a little when she calls me out for being a bitch to Tyler. I mean, I know I can generally be a difficult person and I know that sometimes I'm not very nice to Tyler, but I don't think I'm a bitch when it comes to him, am I? He gives as good as he gets, so it never feels like I'm truly being horrible to him. Now that I think about what's going on his life, I actually feel bad for him.

Charlotte called me earlier and told me that Tyler showed up at her and Gavin's house having a meltdown because he found out his dad wasn't really his dad. I feel sorry for him, really I do. I just know that if I'm anywhere near him, I'm going to want to have sex with him. It's like a sickness. I think I need a Tyler Twelve Step Program. Or shock therapy.

"Fine. What's the plan? And where is he anyway?" I ask.

"He sort of jumped into the shower fully clothed. Gavin is getting him some dry clothes to put on. We don't really have a plan other than getting him drunk to cheer him up. I wouldn't normally suggest this, but maybe you could throw him a bone. Give him a little action. That would make him really happy," Charlotte suggests.

"I'm sorry, but did I just enter the fucking Twilight Zone? You can't stand Tyler! You've been telling me for months that I need to stay away from him," I remind her.

"I know, I know. It's just...I've never seen him like this. I feel awful for him. I know I told you I'd help you find a new guy, but maybe we should hold off on that for right now. Tyler really likes you and it might push him over the edge. I already called and cancelled your blind date for tonight."

Great. Now that my sister is on Team Tyler, I'm never going to be able to quit him.

With a sigh, I get up from the couch and head into the kitchen. I start opening cupboards and pulling out bottles of liquor, lining them up on the counter. If we're going to do this, we're doing it right. Maybe if I get Tyler drunk enough, he'll act like an idiot and I won't be tempted to rip his clothes off.

"I don't think I understand the game of this object. The game of this game. Fuck! I don't think I should have any more vodka," Charlotte slurs.

I've lost count of how many shots we've taken in the last hour. We decided to watch The Kardashians and take a drink every time one of them said 'like'. Gavin is trying to get us to play a different game now.

I watch from my spot on the loveseat as Charlotte curls into Gavin's side on the couch and he wraps his arm around her, pulling her close. Looking over at Tyler sitting on the floor in front of them with his chin resting on the coffee table, I wonder what it would be like to have the kind of relationship that Charlotte and Gavin have. They're so in love it's disgusting, but it's also kind of nice. They always have someone to talk to and lean on. They have a best friend in each other and someone to come home to every day. Maybe I've been too hard on Tyler.

"I think we should play 'Ava lets Tyler stick it in her ass'!" Tyler shouts excitedly.

Never mind.

"Exit only, moron," I remind him.

"I let Gavin have anal. You should try it, Ava. It's gooooooood," Charlotte says with a laugh.

I can't help but cringe. Seriously, there are just some things you should not know about your sister.

"See? Charlotte likes it. You should give it a try. Gavin, can we borrow your bedroom and a stick of butter?" Tyler asks, looking over his shoulder at Gavin.

"What the hell do you need butter for?" Gavin replies.

"Um, duh, for lube."

Gavin reaches for the bottle of vodka on the coffee table and pours four shots. "Moving right along. Okay, here's how this game works. Someone starts off by saying a phrase. It can be anything you want, no more than a couple of words. Everyone else has to scream that phrase as loud as they can without laughing. If you laugh, you take a shot."

"This sounds too easy and like no one will be drinking the rest of the night," I tell him.

"That's what you think. I am the master of this game," Tyler adds. "I'll go first."

The room is silent while he sits there thinking for a few minutes.

I'm about ready to complain that he's taking too long and my buzz is wearing off when he suddenly says, "Dick nipples."

We all stare down at him and then at each other, before we scream at the top of our lungs.

"DICK NIPPLES!"

Charlotte is the first to lose it, naturally. She starts laughing hysterically before she even gets to the word *nipples*.

"Down the hatch, baby!" Gavin tells her with a laugh, handing her a shot.

She tosses it back, half of it dribbling down her chin.

"Alright, since Charlotte lost, it's her turn," Tyler tells her, getting up from the floor and walking over to the loveseat. He sits down next to me, resting his arm on the back of the couch, his fingers brushing my shoulder.

It could be the vodka, but I suddenly feel really warm. I move as far away from him on the cushions as I can, but there's not very far for me to go. Who the fuck made loveseats so small? I can't really get up and move without letting him know he has some sort of effect on me.

Fuck you, hormones.

"ANGRY UTERUS!" Charlotte suddenly yells.

"Seriously, that's what you're going with?" I ask her. "And I don't think you're the one who is supposed to shout it."

"ANGRY UTERUS, ANGRY UTERUS, ANGRY FUCKING UTERUS!" she screams, bouncing up and down on the couch excitedly.

Once again, we all look at each other before shouting it back. This time, Tyler is the one who loses.

"Sorry, I couldn't help it. I just keep picturing a uterus with tiny little fists of fury screaming at people in a chipmunk voice, 'I'm a wee little uterus and I will fuck all of you up.'" Tyler says in a high-pitch voice before taking his shot.

I giggle and then clamp my hand over my mouth.

Jesus Christ, I don't giggle. What the hell is wrong with me? Tyler isn't funny. Tyler is annoying.

I feel the tips of his fingers graze my shoulder again and this time I shiver. Glancing over at him, I see him smirk and it takes everything in me not to reach over and smack him.

Fuck, why does he have to look so good? And smell good, too.

He's taller than me when I wear heels, which immediately goes in the 'plus' column. He's got blonde, surfer-boy hair that is long enough for me to grab onto, but not so long that he needs to put it in a ponytail. That's a deal breaker for me. If you need to borrow one of my ponytail holders, you need to pack up your vagina and leave. He's not big and beefy in the muscles department, but he's definitely cut. I've run my hands over his six-pack plenty of times. If he shaved every day, he'd have a baby face, but with the stubble he's always sporting, that face jumps right up into man territory. And good God, does that stubble feel good when it rubs up against my thighs…

"Alright, dude, it's your turn," Gavin tells Tyler, breaking me out of my fantasy.

I watch in horror as Charlotte moves her hand down to Gavin's crotch.

"We should go have some sex," she attempts to whisper in his ear.

I roll my eyes and take my shot.

"Hey, I didn't even say my phrase yet," Tyler complains as I slam my empty glass onto the coffee table and pour myself another.

Thankfully, the vodka starts to make my vision blur and I can easily ignore my sister as she continues to fondle Gavin through his jeans.

"Big dick titty fucker," Tyler states.

Gavin and Charlotte immediately start laughing before we even have a chance to repeat Tyler's choice phrase. They both do their shot and then Gavin stands up suddenly, pulling Charlotte with him.

"Alright, game's over. My dick has somewhere it needs to be," Gavin laughs.

Tyler and I stare after the two of them as they run from the room and down the hall, their bedroom door slamming closed behind them.

We sit here on the couch listening to laughter and moans coming from the bedroom, and after a few minutes, it starts to get really awkward. I do NOT need to listen to my sister having sex.

"So, what do you want to do?" Tyler asks.

Without thinking about what I'm doing, I push myself up, swing my leg over his thigh and straddle his lap, clutching onto handfuls of his hair.

"This is a one-time thing and I'm only doing this because I feel sorry about what happened to you today," I tell him honestly.

His hands grab onto my ass and he pulls me down against him, lifting his hips at the same time so that I can feel how hard he is.

"I can live with that," he replies.

Pulling his face closer, I crash my lips to his and pray to God that once my buzz wears off I'll forget this ever happened.

CHAPTER 6

Accidental Anal

- Tyler -

"Oh, my God. You're so wet and tight and-"

"Shut up. Stop talking," Ava pants as I pound into her from behind.

It's probably wrong that I've got her bent over the arm of the couch in my best friend's living room, but I don't give a fuck. If this is wrong, I don't wanna be right. I should still be freaking out about the bombshell my parents dropped on me this morning or the fact that Ava is only doing this because she pities me, but I don't have time for that right now. I've been dreaming about being inside of her again and I'm determined not to think about anything else.

My pants are around my thighs and Ava's skirt is bunched up around her waist. We didn't bother taking our clothes off out of courtesy for Gavin and Charlotte. Sure, we're defiling their couch right now, but at least we're being considerate by not being *naked* on their couch.

"You're pussy is like a warm Christmas cookie, fresh from the oven," I mutter as I slam into her harder.

"Jesus Christ, STOP TALKING! Oh, my God, harder," Ava demands.

I close my eyes and let my head fall back as I give her what she wants. God, she is such a bitch. I don't know what it is about her, but I just can't stay away from her. She hates me and I kind of can't stand her, but holy fuck is the sex good with her.

I can feel my balls start to tighten and I know I'm going to come any second. I know I should slow down and savor what could be my last time with Ava, but I can't. Her moans are getting louder and it just turns me on even more. She screams my name and smacks her hands down on the couch as she comes, which just throws me over the edge. Usually, she calls me 'mother fucker' or 'dick face,' so the sound of my name on her lips as she orgasms is enough to make me completely lose my shit. My hips are moving so fast against her ass that the couch starts sliding across the living room floor and, with one last thrust, I start coming. I'm completely oblivious to what I'm doing because it feels so fucking good.

That was my first mistake.

Wait for it.

"SON OF A MOTHER FUCKING BITCH!" Ava screams suddenly and I feel her entire body go rigid before she pulls away from me and scrambles over the arm of the couch.

I can tell by the sound of her voice that this is not a passion-filled 'son of a mother fucking bitch, I'm coming again' scream. It's more of a 'son of a fucking bitch, I'm going to kill you' scream.

It takes me a second to realize what's going on because I'm still in the process of coming, my hips moving all on their own, fucking nothing but air.

My eyes fly open and I find her huddled at the other end of the couch giving me a dirty look.

"What the hell?" I ask in confusion, pulling my pants up from around my thighs.

"What the hell? YOU PUT YOUR DICK IN MY ASS!" she screams.

I open the waist of my pants and glance down at my condom-covered dick in wonder, half expecting him to look up at me and wink for that sweet ninja move he pulled.

Holy shit, I just had anal!

I raise my eyebrows and smile.

Second mistake.

"This is NOT funny. Wipe that Goddamn smile off of your face RIGHT NOW! I was saving anal for my future husband!" she yells at me before reaching for one of the empty vodka bottles on the coffee table and chucking it at my head.

"JESUS CHRIST!" I yell, ducking down behind the arm of the couch just in time as the bottle goes sailing over me and *thumps* against the side of the island in the kitchen.

"It was a mistake, I swear." I raise my hands above my head and wave them back and forth like a white flag of peace. "Either you have a really tight vagina, or a really loose asshole because I didn't even notice."

Mistake número tres. In case you weren't keeping track.

She screams like a banshee and I have just enough time to wrap my arms around my head before she dives over my end of the couch and starts smacking every inch of face she can reach.

"I'm sorry! Jesus, I'm sorry. Stop hitting me! It was an honest mistake!"

"HONEST MISTAKE?!" she screeches. "An honest mistake is speeding, spilling a glass of milk or calling someone by the wrong name. It is NOT sticking your dick in the wrong hole!" she argues, her fist connecting with my cheek.

In between grunts of pain, I manage to grab onto her wrists and stand up. Her hair is a mess around her face and her cheeks are red from exertion and even though I'm pretty sure I should excuse myself to get rid of the jizz-filled condom I'm still wearing, I can feel myself getting hard again.

She tries to struggle out of my grasp but I hold on tight as I climb over the arm of the couch and push her onto her back on the cushions, resting my body on top of hers. Holding her arms above her head, I stare down at her face and try really hard to wipe the goofy smile off of my mine.

I don't know what she's so worked up about. It really *was* an honest mistake. There's only like a one-inch distance between the two holes. It could happen to anyone.

"You know, since I was already in there…"

Yep, you guessed it. I should probably just stop talking.

I may have her hands pinned, but her legs are still in working order. Her knee comes up between my legs and slams right into my balls.

I let out a scream and roll right off of her and onto the floor, clutching onto the boys as I curl up in the fetal position.

In between whimpers of pain, I watch as Ava gets up off of the couch and storms around the living room, picking up random objects: a shot glass, an empty bottle of vodka, the remote control and a huge jar candle. She cradles everything in her arms and then stalks over to me.

"I don't think Charlotte and Gavin expect you to clean up the living room," I groan, pushing myself up from the floor gingerly and wincing when it feels like my nut sack is going to explode.

"Oh, I'm not cleaning up. I'm going to shove these things up your ass and see how you like it," she tells me.

"I told you I was sorry," I remind her, using the edge of the couch to push myself up from the ground.

"We are never having sex again!"

I laugh and, with my hands cupping my balls, I start walking down the hall to Gavin and Charlotte's bathroom to dispose of the condom. I'm definitely too drunk to drive back to my parent's house. Hopefully Gavin and Charlotte won't mind if I crash here.

"You said that last week, Ava. Admit it, you can't get enough of me."

I hear her curse and I can't help but laugh as I use a wad of toilet paper to remove the condom and throw it in the trash before hobbling into the bedroom.

This day started off shitty and even though I can almost feel my balls up in my throat after that kick Ava gave me, it still ended on a good note. I kind of, sort of popped my anal cherry. Technically, I guess I popped *her* anal cherry, but semantics…I feel like I should tell someone about this. Is this the type of thing you post on Facebook or send out a mass text about? If not, it should be.

Tomorrow, I'm going to think about the fact that the man I grew up with isn't my father and pray my parents aren't hurt when I tell them I need to find out who he is. I have to know where I came from. Not just because it's imperative that I have an official birth certificate, but also because I need to know if my dad was a turkey baster or some asshole who slept with my mom and then never spoke to her again. When I do find out who he is, I'm going to beat his ass.

Climbing into bed, I slide my hands behind my head and stare up at the ceiling.

I have no idea who my father is.

I just had anal!

But I have no idea who my father is.

ANAL, MOTHER FUCKER!

Shit, I hate being so conflicted.

CHAPTER 7

Ass Captain

~ Ava ~

As soon as the photo loads to the page, I do a quick preview of my blog post and smile. Something Charlotte said to me the other day when we went shopping struck a chord. She called me the Rain Man of fashion. Ever since I was a little girl I have always been obsessed with clothes and shoes, purses and jewelry. I would take playing dress-up to the extreme, reorganizing my mom's closet and putting outfits together for her for an entire year.

Everyone has a blog nowadays. They talk about their lives, their kids, and whatever else they have going on and it's all the same boring crap day after day. I've had a blog for a while and I rarely post on it. When I do, it's always about an outfit I wore or a sale I found at the mall and I always get a ton of hits, so I've decided to test something out and see where it goes. I'm starting an official fashion blog. I'll keep people up-to-date on current trends and where all the good sales are and post photos of myself wearing certain items so they can see how I pair things together. It's not something I'll be able to make a living doing, but at least it's something I'm excited about.

I hit 'publish' on the blog post and, while I wait for it to go live, my cell phone rings. When I see that it's my mom, I groan before answering it.

"There better be a damn good reason why you called off of work today," mom says, not bothering with 'hello'.

Letting out a little cough, I make my voice sound as weak as possible. "I'm really sick, Mom. Like, really. I think it's the flu."

She sighs through the line and I watch with a smile on my face as the views on my blog post already start adding up within seconds of it going live.

"Bullshit. You've been on your computer since dinner last night. In case you've forgotten, I know how to work the Internet. I just saw your blog post go live. Did you seriously call off of work to play around on your blog? You're messing up a perfectly good career opportunity, Ava. Even though I'm part owner of the company, I can't continue to cover for you when you do stupid shit like this," she complains.

I feel the butterflies of excitement about my blog post die a quick, painful death in my stomach when she calls what I'm doing 'stupid shit'. I love my mom, but she's never understood the fact that I don't want to be part of the family business, that I have other likes and interests apart from hers. I feel the sting of tears in my eyes and I have to squeeze them tightly closed to keep the tears from falling. No matter what I do, I just can't make her understand how important this is to me.

"I expect you to be back at work first thing tomorrow morning," she adds. "And for God's sake, call Tyler. He's decided that every time you ignore one of his voicemails or texts, he's going to forward them to me. Remember that song 'Accidentally in Love' from *Shrek*? Well, there is now a five-minute voicemail on my phone of him singing it, but he changed the lyrics to 'Accidentally in Your Ass.' I really do not need to know what *that* is about. Make him stop."

For right now, I decide the best thing is to just agree with my mom. If I try to explain to her once again how much I hate working at Seduction and Snacks, I'll never hear the end of it.

I hang up with my mom and scroll through all of the text messages from Tyler. He's been sending them to me non-stop for five days. Five days since he violated my ass. Okay, fine, it was an accident. I know he really didn't do it on purpose; he's not that kind of guy. He wouldn't just try to sneak his dick in there and figure I wouldn't notice.

Okay, he probably would, but he would be honest about doing it once I called him on it. He was adamant that it was a mistake and I'm pissed off that I believe him. I'm even more pissed off that, after the initial shock wore off, I was sorely tempted to demand he grab some lube and keep going.

As I read each message, I'm ashamed at myself for cracking a tiny smile.

I need to ASS you a question. Are you still mad at me?

Dear Ava's Ass: I'm sorry. Please forgive me.
Love, Tyler's Ginormous Dick.

I bought a butt plug. You're right. This isn't very comfortable.

Never mind. This isn't so bad.

"I'm in love (with your ass), I'm in love (with your ass).
Come on, come on, spin a little tighter" Wow, these lyrics are
spot on. I think I found our new theme song.
Check your voice mail.

With a growl, I wipe the smile off of my face and finally reply to all of Tyler's nonsense.

STOP TEXTING ME AND FOR FUCK'S SAKE,
STOP TEXTING AND CALLING MY MOM!

He replies immediately, asking me if I've forgiven him yet and it makes me wonder if he's been sitting there for five days with his phone in his hand waiting for me to respond. This just makes me angrier because I kind of like the idea of a guy waiting around for me. I just don't like the idea that it's *Tyler* doing the waiting. He needs to go away.

Tossing my phone on my bed, I abandon my blog post, no longer as excited about it as I was, and make my way into the kitchen. Even though I'm not keen on being a part of the family business, I still like the things that are part of that business, namely, baking. I pull out all of the ingredients I need and get busy making some cupcakes. They say the way to a man's heart is through his stomach. I certainly don't want anywhere near Tyler's heart, but maybe a few dozen cupcakes dusted with rat poison will finally make him realize I don't want him.

The first batch of cupcakes is on a rack cooling and I'm whipping up some frosting, when I hear the front door open. Glancing up from the mixing bowl, I see my Aunt Claire walk into the room.

"I smelled baked goods as soon as I pulled in the driveway. Ooooh, cupcakes. What kind?" she asks, coming around the counter and bending down to look in the oven.

My Aunt Claire isn't really my aunt, just my mom's long-time best friend and business partner. She's the one who runs the sweet side of Seduction and Snacks and she taught me everything I know about baking.

"Chocolate chip cookie dough cupcakes with chocolate ganache icing," I tell her as I turn off the mixer and grab a spatula.

"Alright, out with it," Aunt Claire tells me as she turns around and perches on one of the bar stools across the counter from me.

"Out with what?" I ask her innocently, making sure not to make eye contact.

"You only bake when someone pisses you off or you're upset

about something, so spill. Who pissed in your Cheerios?"

I should have known that Aunt Claire would realize something was wrong as soon as she walked in the door. She practically raised me and can read me like a book.

"Several people have pissed me off lately. My 'People to Kill' list has grown by leaps and bounds in the past few weeks," I admit.

"Well, that's nothing new. You hate people. Be more specific," she tells me, swiping her finger into the bowl of frosting and bringing it to her mouth. "Add a teaspoon of almond extract to that."

Turning away from her, I reach into the spice cabinet above the stove and grab the almond. I'm not really ready to discuss how disappointed I am in my mom for not understanding my future career choices with anyone, but especially not my mom's best friend. If I asked her to, she would keep my secret, but I don't want to have to put her in the position of keeping something from her best friend, so I go with the easier target.

"Tyler. He's gotten a little taste of the Amazing Ava and now he won't go away," I joke, adding the almond to the frosting and mixing it in.

"I'm assuming that's why you have six boxes of chocolate-flavored laxatives sitting here next to the container of sugar?" Aunt Claire asks, lifting up one of the boxes and raising her eyebrows at me.

I shrug. "We didn't have any rat poison. I figure if he's shitting his brains out he'll be too busy to bug me."

Aunt Claire gets up from the stool and starts rummaging

through the pantry until she finds what she needs. With her arms full of pastry bags, decorator tips and pre-made frosting, she comes back to the counter and dumps everything on top.

"I'm going to kick your mom's ass for buying this shit frosting in a tub, but it will save us some time," Aunt Claire tells me as she scoops some of the vanilla frosting from the tub into a pastry bag and adds the standard round tip to the end of it.

"Let's give Tyler's ass a break and do something a lot more fun," Aunt Claire tells me.

I start to say something about how he didn't give *my* ass a break, but I'm not ready to get into that with her, either. I watch over her shoulder as she begins piping words onto the cupcakes. Her handwriting with frosting is flawless and beautiful, even with the words she's chosen to adorn the top of the cupcakes.

I read them out loud, confused a little at the last one. "Smelly crotch, dick biscuit, taint licker…shart fucker?"

Aunt Claire pauses and moves the pastry bag away from the cupcake. "Yeah, I'm running out of ideas."

She continues writing random things on the cupcakes and we're both silent for a few minutes as I watch her work, putting as much concentration into these cupcakes as she does with a wedding cake she makes for a stranger.

After a little while, she finally breaks the silence. "You know, Tyler might be immature, but he does have a little bit of sweetness in him, even if it's kind of fucked up. He's loyal to a fault and will do anything for one of his friends. Plus, his mom's more of a slut than your mom, so there's that."

I can't help but laugh and I'm thankful that my aunt decided to stop by. I still need to end things with Tyler once and for all, but maybe I can stop being such a bitch to him. After I give him these cupcakes, of course.

Aunt Claire finishes the last one, pulling back to examine her masterpieces. "There, all done. I have to stop by Seduction and Snacks after this. Want me to hand deliver them?" she asks.

I nod my head, my eyes zeroing in on the last cupcake. I quickly snatch it from the counter. "Yes, but not this one. He can't have this one."

She watches in shock as I shove the entire thing in my mouth. "Hey, that was my favorite one! What's wrong with Ass Captain?"

CHAPTER 8

Pinky Pleasure or Butt Tower

- Tyler -

"Tyler, what the hell are you doing?"

Looking up from the mess surrounding me, I see Gavin standing at the end of the aisle where I'm currently sitting on the floor. It's the end of my first week at Seduction and Snacks and really, I should be ecstatic. Every tour I did of the warehouse went smoothly, I answered all the questions thrown at me expertly and I started up a competition with the warehouse workers that's already starting to boost morale. I'm going to have to set a few ground rules for Vibrator Sword Fight Fridays so we don't almost lose an eye again, but other than that, I'm pleased with my performance. Shoving a handful of ice cubes into the penis-shaped pillow we carry went a long way towards calming Scott Jameson down after the Racing Rocket came close to making him a Cyclops. Obviously the penis pillow didn't make him happy, but we don't carry a vagina pillow. The ice brought down the swelling on his eye and he promised not to sue us for assault with a deadly weapon.

Unfortunately, I can't stop thinking about the fact that Ava won't return my calls or that I might find out today who my dad is.

"Well, Gavin, I'm sitting on the floor surrounded by vibrators and pocket pussies. Obviously I'm trying to think," I tell him, lying down on my back in the middle of the pile and swiping my arms and legs against the floor.

"Are you making a dildo angel?" Gavin asks, walking down the aisle until he's standing right next to me.

I sit back up and carefully stand, making sure not to disrupt my masterpiece. Jumping over the toys on the floor, I stand next to Gavin and we stare down at my pretty dildo angel.

"I heard you talked to my Aunt Liz about the whole birth certificate thing," he finally says.

"Yep. She told me to take my time getting her the real thing and that she'd pay me under the table until then."

I thought for sure Ava's mom was going to fire my ass when I told her I couldn't get her a copy of my birth certificate for the employment forms. She just smiled at me and told me not to worry about it, which is very unlike her. Obviously either Tyler or Ava had already explained the situation to her and she felt sorry for me. Awesome. Yet another person who pities me. I didn't mind it so much the other night with Ava because it meant she'd sleep with me. I don't like everyone else looking at me like I'm some sad, pathetic, fatherless dude.

"Did you tell your parents you called the sperm bank to have them pull the records?"

I nod and we turn to walk away from my angel, making our way into the offices. "I had to. The place wouldn't release any personal information unless my mom went in and signed a few papers saying she was okay with me finding out who my dad is. They're supposed to call me today with the guy's name and phone number so I can contact him."

Unfortunately, they can only give me the name of the guy who donated the sperm. That doesn't mean he's my real father since my mom was a slut.

Goddammit!

We walk into the break room and take a seat at the table.

"And how do you feel about that?" Gavin asks.

The thing about Gavin is, he's a genuinely good guy no matter how much I've tried to corrupt him. He's always been a good friend and I know he's worried about my mental health right now, but I don't feel like hashing this out with anyone. I just want to get this thing over with, find out who my dad is and beat the shit out of him. Then, I can go on with my life and never have to think about the guy ever again.

"Can we stop pretending like we have vaginas? I don't want to talk about my feelings, Dr. Phil. How about we talk about the fact that I got anal the other night at your house," I tell him proudly, leaning back in my chair and clasping my hands behind my head.

"Correction, you *accidentally* had anal and you barely got the tip in. You're forgetting that you're sleeping with my girlfriend's sister.

They tell each other everything," Gavin laughs.

"Whatever. My dick still went into a hole that has been previously denied me. I don't care how much of it went in, it still went in. And she baked me cupcakes as a thank you."

Gavin shakes his head at me. "You mean the cupcakes that called you a Piss Drinker and a Turtle Fucker? I'm pretty sure that wasn't her saying thank you. That was her saying that none of her holes will be welcoming you inside anytime soon."

I wave my hand at him. "Mere technicalities."

The door to the break room opens and Gavin's dad, Carter, walks in with Ava's dad, Jim. Liz and Claire have to conduct a huge production meeting every Friday, so their husbands always stop by to pick them up and take them to dinner afterwards.

"Your mom said you boys might be in here. She and Liz have a few things to finish up before they're ready to go. How was work?" Carter asks as he pulls out a chair and takes a seat next to Gavin while Jim does the same next to me.

I've always liked Carter and Jim, even though Jim scares me sometimes. He's a quiet man, but I have a feeling if he knew the things I've done to his daughter, he'd chop off my balls and make me eat them. Gavin is a really great guy, treats Charlotte like a queen and he still punched Gavin in the face when he found out Gavin was in love with Charlotte. If he finds out his daughter has had intimate knowledge of my penis and I've secretly snuck in her bedroom on a few occasions, he will straight up murder my ass.

"Work was good. We were just talking about anal sex, care to add to the discussion?" Gavin tells them with a laugh.

I shoot him the middle finger and give him the stink eye. Jesus Christ, this is not something that should be discussed with Ava's dad two feet away from me. He's within punching distance.

"If you asking about anal sex has anything to do with my daughter, I think you should know that I'm perfectly fine with spending my life in prison," Jim warns him.

I gulp nervously and slide my chair a few inches away from Jim. The closer I am to the door, the easier it will be for me to run the fuck out of here if he finds out about me and Ava.

"Remember the words you're supposed to say to me whenever we're in the same room together?" Jim continues.

Gavin nods his head and speaks in a monotone voice like he's reading from a cue card. "Charlotte and I are waiting until marriage and we have separate bedrooms. We only kiss on Sundays after church and a thorough reading of the Bible."

Jim smiles in satisfaction and relaxes in his chair.

"Well, I myself don't care for anal that much, but Claire is pretty gung-ho about the whole thing," Carter admits, bringing the conversation back around.

"Oh, Jesus Christ, I didn't think this thing through. Stop it, stop it right now," Gavin tells him, covering his ears with his hands and cringing.

I can't help but laugh. He asked for it, thinking he could out me in front of Ava's dad. Now he has to deal with the image of his mom and dad having butt sex. Serves him right.

"If you have enough lube and porn on the television, anything is possible," Jim adds.

"I find that olive oil works much better," Carter explains, placing his elbows on the table and leaning forward.

"I CAN'T HEAR YOU! LA-LA-LA, I'M NOT LISTENING!" Gavin screams with his hands still over his ears.

The men ignore him and since I've got a couple of experts at my disposal, I, too, lean forward and suck in all of their knowledge like a sponge.

"Tell me about this olive oil thing you speak of," I say to Carter.

"Well, olive oil is a natural lubricant, it's good for your skin and it's always handy. However, you can't use it with condoms because it will break down the rubber and make them less effective," Carter explains.

Noticing a notepad and pen in the middle of the table, I grab both of them and slide them towards me. This is too good not to take notes. I start scribbling furiously as Carter and Jim go back and forth.

"Also, lots of alcohol. Liz is always more adventurous after a bottle of wine. We prefer Anal Eaze. It has a numbing agent that works wonders," Jim mentions, grabbing the pen out of my hand and adding that to my list of notes.

"No, no, no. You can't use that shit," Carter interrupts. "If she's numb, she has no idea if your tiny penis is hurting her. She has to feel what's going on so she can tell you to stop."

"LONDON BRIDGE IS FALLING DOWN, FALLING DOWN, FALLING DOWN. LONDON BRIDGE IS FALLING DOWN, MY FAIR LADY!" Gavin screams.

Everyone ignores him.

"Tiny penis, ha! Even after twenty some odd years together, Liz still walks funny after we have sex," Jim admits.

"That's because you're doing it wrong and probably fucked her thigh instead of her vagina," Carter laughs.

"What about you guys? Has either of you ever taken it up the ass?" I ask.

They stop their verbal sparring and stare at me like I'm insane. I don't see what the big deal is; it's a good question.

"I mean honestly, how can you know if what you're doing is any good if you don't experience it yourself?" I ask.

"Tyler, are you gay?" Carter asks.

"No! I'm not gay, I'm just saying. A little equal opportunity goes a long way when you're trying to get your woman to give you something she wouldn't normally. I am man enough to admit that I stuck a little something up my ass, and it wasn't so bad."

Jim stares down in horror at the pen in his hand that he took from me and then suddenly chucks it across the room. He jumps up from his seat and races over to the sink, dumping half the bottle of liquid soap into his hands before scrubbing them furiously.

I roll my eyes at him. "I didn't stick that pen up my ass, don't worry. You do know that we carry a very nice line of butt plugs here at Seduction and Snacks, right?"

Gavin lowers his hands from his ears. "Dude, seriously? Are we talking Pinky Pleasure or Butt Tower? Because there is a huge difference between those sizes."

"Bigger than a Q-Tip and smaller than a bread basket," I tell him with a smile.

"Huh. You might be on to something," Carter says, with a thoughtful expression on his face. "What aisle are butt plugs on again?"

Gavin screams, throwing his hands up over his ears.

"Wait a minute, are you asking all of these questions out of general curiosity or are you sleeping with someone?" Jim asks, drying his hands on a paper towel.

Don't look suspicious, don't look suspicious.

"Oh, you know, just keeping my options open. Hey, is that Liz? Hi, Liz!" I shout, looking through the glass doors next to Jim and waving at no one.

Jim doesn't turn around; he just narrows his eyes at me.

"I swear to all that is holy, if I find out this has anything to do with Ava, I will shove my fist up your ass," he threatens.

"Whoa, slow down there, Jim. I'm only on butt plugs. I'm not quite ready for fisting yet."

Carter leans closer to Jim. "I've got a better idea. How about we just unleash Cougar Claire on him as punishment?"

Jim gives me a sinister look and I feel a bead of sweat run down my back. Having a crush on Claire since college and always shooting perverted innuendos her way did not end well for me a few months ago. It's one thing to have a Mrs. Robinson fantasy about your best friend's mom in your spank bank, but it's something straight out of a fucking horror movie when she decides to act on it.

The sweet nothings she whispered in my ear quickly turned to threats about making me part of the next Human Centipede movie if I didn't cut that shit out. Now, whenever she walks in the room, I have PTSD flashbacks of that day in her house when she made me clean the kitchen floor on my hands and knees and then had me hand wash her period panties with the garden hose out back to teach me a lesson about flirting with older women.

Lesson learned.

Before Jim can threaten me any more, my phone rings. Reaching into the pocket of my jeans, I pull it out and check the display, swallowing nervously when I see it's the sperm bank calling me back.

Gavin notices the look on my face and slowly lowers his hands from his ears as I answer the call.

"Uh-huh. Yep. Sure. Okey dokey, thanks."

Ending the call, I set my phone on the table in front of me and stare at it.

"They found out who my dad is and he wants to meet me tomorrow at noon," I whisper.

Suddenly, getting fisted by Ava's dad sounds a whole lot more appealing.

CHAPTER 9

Dolphin Rape

~ Ava ~

"I want this blog to look really professional and, since you handle all of the media and design stuff for the Seduction and Snacks website, I thought you might be able to help me out."

Sliding my laptop across the table towards Aunt Jenny, I wait nervously as she scrolls through a couple of my posts.

Out of everyone, I figure Aunt Jenny would be the most supportive of my idea. She thinks everything is a good idea, even if she doesn't understand it most of the time.

"I don't get it. Is this going to be a porn site? You've got a bunch of pictures of your clothes all over your bed. Is that a Hermès scarf? Oh, please don't tell me you want to have sex on a Hermès," Aunt Jenny groans.

Closing my eyes, I take a deep breath and try to explain this to her again. "No, Aunt Jenny, this is not a porn site. I'm giving people fashion tips and stuff like that."

Uncle Drew walks into the dining room a few minutes later while Aunt Jenny is still staring in confusion at my webpage.

"Hey, baby, do these jeans make my butt look big?" he asks, turning around and sticking his ass out.

Aunt Jenny looks up and smiles. "No, but they make your penis look stupidest."

I groan and shake my head at her. "I think you mean stupendous and that's just gross."

Uncle Drew walks over to Aunt Jenny and leans down to kiss her cheek before checking out what's on the computer. "Thanks, babe. Hey, are you looking at porn without me? Where's the chick who took all those clothes off?"

I huff and cross my arms in front of me in irritation. "It is NOT a fucking porn site!"

Uncle Drew ignores me and reaches over Aunt Jenny's shoulder to click through some of the pictures. "I don't get it. Why aren't there any chicks in these photos? Oh, hey, there's Ava! Wait, are you doing porn? Your parents are NOT going to be happy about this."

Why did I think coming here was a good idea?

"I can definitely add some graphics to your blog and make it look nicer," Aunt Jenny tells me. "To be honest though, I think porn might be a better idea. You could totally make a lot of money doing that. I don't think anyone is going to pay just to look at your clothes and stuff. Ooooh, you should make some videos of you taking your clothes OFF instead of just having pictures of your clothes lying around AFTER you took them off. People would totally pay to see that."

"I would pay to see that," Uncle Drew adds.

"Eeeeew, seriously?" I ask in disgust.

"Dude, not you. That's just gross," he reassures me. "But Jenny? Totally. You should put Jenny on your site taking her clothes off. I've already got a few good shots of her ass on my cell phone I can send you."

He pulls his cell phone out of the back pocket of his jeans and starts scrolling through his pictures. "Oh, man, I forgot about this one. Remember when we rented the dolphin costume and recorded that public service announcement?"

Aunt Jenny forgets about my site and her face lights up. "Yes! The pasa! That was so much fun!"

"What's a pasa?" I ask in confusion, looking back and forth between them.

"She means PSA," Uncle Drew tells me.

"Right. PSA. It's pronounced pasa," Aunt Jenny adds.

"It's not pronounced anything, babe. It's just called a PSA. It's an acronym," Uncle Drew explains.

"Do I even want to ask what this dolphin PSA is about?"

Uncle Drew sits down at the table next to Aunt Jenny and looks at me seriously. "It's an epidemic that is spreading far and wide. People just have no idea what is happening right under their noses. It's scary and dangerous and they need to be aware. Jenny and I took it upon our selves to educate the world. I can't believe you haven't seen the video. It's been all over YouTube."

Aunt Jenny nods and grabs Uncle Drew's hands. "We read an article about it online and we just knew we had to do something. So, we made a video talking about the dangers of dolphin rape and we posted it online. We've received a ton of messages from people thanking us for our information."

"I'm sorry, did you say *dolphin rape?* Like, what? Dolphins raping other dolphins?" I ask in confusion.

I know I'm going to regret asking this.

"What? No! That would just be silly. Ava, this is about dolphins raping people. Surely you've heard the news," Uncle Drew adds.

"Every ninety-six seconds someone else is raped by a dolphin. Innocent men and women just enjoying a day at the beach and then BAM! A dolphin latches on and doesn't let go. They may seem like sweet and innocent creatures but let me tell you, they are not," Aunt Jenny says with a shiver.

Uncle Drew reaches over and wraps his arm around her shoulders, pulling her in close. "Your aunt had a close call with a dolphin last year on vacation. She doesn't like to talk about it very much."

"It was the worst day of my life," Aunt Jenny wails, burying her face in Uncle Drew's shoulder.

Every day I wonder how in the hell my parents became friends with Aunt Jenny and Uncle Drew. Today, I am completely baffled.

"Um, wow. That's... I don't even know what to say about that," I tell them, completely at a loss for words.

"It's okay, not many people know how to handle a situation like this. It's why we started D.R.A.W. It's a place where people like your Aunt Jenny can meet once a week and talk about their horrific experiences," Uncle Drew explains.

"And D.R.A.W. would stand for…." I prompt, even though I know I'm going to regret it.

"Dolphin Rape Awareness Workshop," Aunt Jenny finishes for me. "Although the meetings don't take place in a workshop. We just couldn't think of another word that started with W."

I'm not sure my brain can take much more information. I really need to bring this conversation back around to my reason for coming here.

"So, anyway. You said you could make some graphics for my site and make it look a little more professional?"

Aunt Jenny pushes away from Uncle Drew and sits up a little straighter. She turns back towards my laptop screen and studies it for a few seconds.

"Sure, no problem. It should only take me a few days. Just write down your password for me," she tells me.

"Well, if you two ladies will excuse me, I have a meeting to get to," Uncle Drew tells us, getting up from his chair and making his way to the front door.

"Meeting? What meeting? You didn't mention that you had a meeting today," Aunt Jenny says as she pushes a piece of paper and a pen towards me so I can write down my log-in information.

"Oh, it's nothing. I just have to see this guy… about a thing. Just… this… thing and a guy with a thing… that I need to see,"

Uncle Drew stammers as he grabs his keys from the side table by their front door.

"Okay, well have a good time!" Aunt Jenny tells him brightly as he rushes out the front door.

I stare at her as she clicks away at my computer. After a few seconds she looks up at me questioningly. "What?"

"He has to see a 'guy' about a 'thing'?" I repeat, using air quotes.

"That's what he said."

I continue to stare at her. "And you don't think that sounds a little bit suspicious?"

"Suspicious how? He knows lots of guys who have things that need to be looked at," she tells me seriously.

I decide to let it go for now, mostly because Uncle Drew isn't here to act as interpreter while I'm talking to Aunt Jenny. I have more important things to worry about right now, like how I can find a way to make money on this website so I can quit working at Seduction and Snacks without giving my mom a heart attack.

CHAPTER 10

I Like Mushrooms

- Tyler -

"Do you want me to come in with you or stay in the car?" Gavin asks as he pulls up to Quick and Delicious, the diner where I'm meeting my...father.

Jesus, it feels so weird so say that.

"Come in. No, stay in the car. Wait, no, come in. SHIT! I don't know what the fuck to do!" I complain as Gavin puts the car in park and shuts off the engine.

"Just take a deep breath, this is going to be fine. Just because you share the same DNA means nothing. Your dad who raised you is still your dad," Gavin reminds me. "Did the company send you that email with his name?"

I grab my phone from the center console and pull up the email app. They sent me an email after we hung up the phone yesterday, but I was too afraid to look at it then.

"This can't be right," I mutter, as I stare at the email from Cryobiology, Inc.

Gavin leans over and glances at the email I pulled up.

"His name is Dean O'Saur? That's got to be a typo," Gavin states.

I close out of the email and open it back up, hoping we both read something wrong.

"Dude, your dad is T-Rex. This may be the best news you've gotten all week!" Gavin says with a laugh.

I groan and throw my head back against the seat.

"T-Rex be like, 'I can't make my bed with these tiny arms'," Gavin says, pulling his elbows into his sides and flapping his hands around.

"This is not funny," I complain.

He continues. "T-Rex be like, 'Raaaawr, that was a good performance, I'm going to clap now. Oh, wait.'"

He continues flailing his hands until I reach over and punch him in the arm.

Gavin finally drops his arms and sighs. "Just don't be a dick right off the bat. It's not like he got drunk and had a one-night-stand with your mom and then didn't speak to her again for like a ton of years."

I look over at him and raise my eyebrow.

"Fuck! I just described MY dad. Well, this sucks," he complains.

"I'm just going to go in there, see if we look anything like one another and then leave," I tell him.

Gavin nods. "Good plan. Get his medical history too. If there's a history of mental illness then at least you know your problems are hereditary, T-Rex, Jr."

"I'm going to drag you out of this car and beat the fuck out of you," I warn him, reaching for the door handle.

With one last fortifying breath, I shove open the door and step out of the car.

"Oh, you should give him some My Little Pony trivia questions. If he gets them wrong, you know he's not really your dad," Gavin shouts as I flip him off before slamming the door closed.

Really, what's the big deal with the fact that I like My Little Pony? I know for a fact I'm not the only one. I Googled it. There's an entire following of people just like me who appreciate that friendship is magic. If Gavin took one second to watch the videos I gave him, he would realize that they are relatable, endearing ponies that have meaningful developments in their lives. If more people liked My Little Pony, world peace wouldn't be an issue, I guarantee it. You just can't watch that show without feeling happy. I also can't watch that show without getting horny.

I walk through the doors of Quick and Delicious, scanning the restaurant for a dude in his forties who looks like me. After a quick glance, I don't see anyone that fits the bill. I walk up to the hostess counter and wait for one of the waitresses to finish cashing someone out.

"Hi, I'm supposed to be meeting someone here. His name is

Dean," I tell her. I refuse to give his full name to anyone ever, even a complete stranger. That shit needs to stay quiet.

She smiles at me as she comes around the counter. "Yep, he's been here for a few minutes. Right this way."

My palms start to sweat and I feel like I'm going to puke as I follow her through the restaurant. I get more and more nervous with each table we walk by and I contemplate turning around and running back out to the car.

Why the hell am I doing this? Gavin is right. Nick Branson is my father, for all intents and purposes. He taught me how to play catch, he bought me my first My Little Pony and he passed down his porn collection to me when I turned eighteen. I couldn't ask for a better father. I shouldn't feel like I don't know who I am just because I suddenly found out the man who raised me doesn't share the same DNA as me. It shouldn't matter.

And yet, it does.

What if I need a kidney transplant and the only match is this guy? What if my sperm doesn't work and the only way I can get my future wife pregnant with a baby who shares my DNA is by using *this* guy's sperm? I have to do this. I have to be strong and do this for the health of my kidneys and for the lives of my future children. It wouldn't be weird at all that their grandfather is also their father, right? I mean, people do that shit all the time and you never hear anyone say, "This is my grandpa-dad" when they're introduced. It will be fine. It will all be just fine.

"Here we go, I'll be right back to take your drink order."

The woman smiles at me and walks away and I get my first

glimpse of my father. He's got the same blonde hair as I do, but that's about the only similarity I see.

The man smiles up at me as I slide into the booth.

"So, you're Dean," I state, breaking the silence after a few seconds.

"I like mushrooms," he replies.

Uh, okay.

"Did you know a female swine will always have an even number of teats? Usually twelve," he adds, the smile never leaving his face.

Thankfully, our waitress comes over and I'm saved from having to comment on pig nipples. She takes our drink orders and leaves us alone again.

"So, thanks for agreeing to see me. I know when you do this sort of thing you never expect to actually meet one of your kids," I tell him with a nervous laugh.

"I like to smell magic markers. Purple is my favorite smell," Dean says, his smile growing even wider.

Oh, my God. They really scraped the bottom of the sperm think tank for my mom, didn't they?

I guess it's random fact time at this Father-Son event.

"Yeah, well, I like to give my balls names that coincide with holidays," I admit, trying to get him to do something other than smile at me.

"Every time you lick a stamp, you consume 1/10 of a calorie. So far today I've had twenty-five calories. I like stamps."

The waitress drops off our drinks and as she turns to leave, I grab onto her arm and pull her close to me.

"Please tell me you made a mistake and sat me at the wrong table," I beg as I whisper in her ear.

She glances across the table and then back at me. "Nope, that's Dean. He was really excited about meeting his son. But just so you know, he's already eaten four paper napkins and he's got one in his hand right now under the table."

She stands up and pats me on the back before walking away again.

"Dean, give me the napkin," I tell him, reaching across the table with my palm up.

He shakes his head at me and frowns.

"Give me the napkin right now. You can't eat napkins, Dean."

I give him a stern look and he slowly lifts his hand out from under the table, a small napkin clutched in his fist. He reaches towards my hand and right when he's about to drop the napkin into it, he quickly pulls his hand back and shoves the entire thing in his mouth.

I stare at him with wide, unblinking eyes as he chews.

"The average human can eat two pounds of paper before risking a bowel obstruction," Dean mumbles through his mouthful of paper.

As the waitress comes back to take our food order, I let my head drop to the table with a *thunk*.

CHAPTER 11
I Will Not Have Sex With Tyler
~ Ava ~

"Look, I told you it's fine with Gavin and I if you stay here until you can find your own place. But do you really think going out and getting drunk tonight is a good idea? You just got in a fight with mom. Maybe you should just stay in. We can pig out on ice cream and watch movies," Charlotte suggests.

I know she means well, but staying here is not going to happen. I'm depressed and pissed off and sitting around watching her and Gavin be all cutesy with one another is just going to push me over the edge.

I ignore her as she sits down on the bed in her guest room while I dig through my suitcase trying to find the perfect outfit for getting tanked and picking up a random stranger at a bar to help take my mind off of things.

I think of Tyler and a flash of guilt washes through me.

Shit! I have no reason to feel guilty. Tyler and I are NOT dating. We have sex every once in a while and, now that I've put an end to it once and for all, I need to get laid and blow off some of this steam. I'm not a slut; I just enjoy sex. Really, really enjoy sex and it's been seven days, thirteen hours and twenty-seven seconds since I last had sex. Not that I'm counting or anything.

"You know mom didn't mean anything that she said today," Charlotte continues as I pull a black, quilted, drop-waist skirt from Forever 21 out of my suitcase and hold it up.

"Do you still have that teal, bow-front, studded tube top from H&M that you wore to Molly's sixteenth birthday party?" I ask about our younger sister, ignoring what Charlotte said about mom.

I made the stupid mistake of showing her the finished blog after Aunt Jenny had worked her magic. I was so excited to show someone how great it looked and she shit all over it, telling me once again that I was wasting my time on something that had nothing to do with my future.

"Dude, seriously? Molly's sixteenth birthday was three years ago. How in the hell do you even remember that?" Charlotte asks.

"Do you still have that top or not? It would look great with this skirt and my black Nine West phantom peep toe ankle boots," I muse.

"It's under the box of dildos."

"JESUS CHRIST!" I shout, jumping in surprise and quickly turning around when I hear Molly's quiet voice.

"How long have you been standing there? And that door was

closed and locked, how did you even get in?" I demand.

I swear to God, Molly should have been a ninja instead of a pastry chef. After being around her for nineteen years, you would think I'd be used to her stealth, but it still catches me off guard. Out of the three of us, she's the most quiet. And I'm not just talking about the way she can move in and out of a room like a ghost. I'm talking about the fact that we don't know anything about her life. She keeps to herself and never shares any personal information, but you can bet your ass she knows everything about everyone else.

Molly just shrugs. "I have my ways. As I was saying, Charlotte still has that shirt. It's on the top shelf of her closet under the largest box of vibrators I've ever seen."

With that little piece of information, she turns and walks out of the room.

"Jesus fuck, she scares me," I mutter before turning back to face Charlotte.

"I swear she can read minds or some shit," Charlotte adds as I pull off my jeans and slip into the skirt. "Did I tell you the other day I was looking all over the place for a twenty-dollar bill that I swore I left on the counter? My phone rang while I was tearing the kitchen apart and when I answered it, all she said was 'It's in the pair of jeans on your bathroom floor' and then she hung up. I think we need to ask mom just how much pot she smoked when she was pregnant with her."

Pulling up the zipper on the side of the skirt, I walk over to the full-length mirror hanging on the wall across the room.

"I'm sure our sister doesn't have special powers. She probably just has your house bugged," I say with a laugh as I check out my reflection. "Now, go get me that shirt. Or do you need some extra muscle to lift that giant box of dildos down off the shelf?"

Charlotte curses at me before getting up from the bed and walking out of the room. She comes back a few minutes later with the top. I slide it on and put the finishing touches on my make-up before blowing her a kiss and telling her not to wait up for me.

"So, what do you say we get out of here? My van is parked outside."

Gulping down the rest of my vodka and Seven, I slam the glass on the top of the bar and turn to face the douche bag sitting next to me.

"Your van? What is this, 1987? Get your hand off of my thigh before I break your fingers," I tell him.

Why did I think going to a bar alone would be a great way to forget about my troubles? As soon as this guy sat down next to me I thought, perfect! A hot guy! And then he opened his mouth.

"Awwww, don't be like that, baby."

Alright, that's it. No one calls me baby.

Clenching my hands, I take a deep breath, not even caring that I'm most likely going to be kicked out of here the moment my fist connects with his face

I turn my body on the barstool right as he lifts up his glass of beer, signaling to the bartender to get him another. He's so drunk that he can't hold his hand steady and the amber liquid in his glass sloshes all over the place while he waves his hand in the air. I watch in horror as beer splashes all over the top of my teal Taylor leather Bette Mini Coach tote.

"You got beer on my Coach," I whisper, unable to take my eyes off of my brand new purse.

"Yo! Bartender! Another beer!" douche bag shouts, completely ignoring me.

"YOU. GOT. BEER. ON. MY. COACH!"

My voice is much louder this time as the rage washes through me. It's one thing for this guy to grope me and talk like a moron, but no one defiles my Coach purse.

"Calm down, baby. It's just a purse-"

My arm flies out before he can even finish his sentence, my elbow connecting with his throat. He drops the glass, both hands flying to his throat and he clutches tightly to it while he coughs and sputters.

"You bitch!" he manages to shout in between coughs.

Before I can even think about threatening to cut off his balls, a hand shoots in between us, grabs onto the front of the guy's shirt and hauls him off of his barstool.

Swiveling around on my seat, I see Tyler pull the guy's face right up to his own and speak in a calm, cool manner.

"Apologize to the lady."

Douche bag looks over at me and gives me a dirty look.

Tyler's hand clutches tighter to the front of the guy's shirt and he roughly yanks him closer. "I said, apologize to the lady, before I shove my knee in your balls."

I should be irritated that Tyler just waltzed in here and took over a situation I could easily handle, but right now, watching him be this big, bad ass protector is making me so hot I can't sit still.

"Sorry," douche bag mumbles.

Tyler shoves the guy away and he stumbles backwards, tripping over his own feet and bumping into a couple of customers. Tyler turns to face me and closes the distance between us, sliding in between my thighs. Without a word to me, he grabs the drink the bartender refilled during the commotion and chugs it. I stare at his throat and watch his Adam's apple bob up and down as he swallows, biting my lip to stop myself from leaning over and licking his skin.

I will not have sex with Tyler, I will not have sex with Tyler.

"So, what's the deal? Were you on a date or something?" he asks, placing the now-empty glass back on the bar.

"Were you following me? I was doing just fine on my own, I didn't need your help," I snap, wincing when I hear how bitchy I sound.

He just shrugs, his hand reaching towards my face. I jerk back right before he touches me and give him a dirty look.

"Relax, princess, I was just going to move a piece of hair off of your cheek."

I hate it when people call me princess. I *really* hate it when Tyler calls me princess. So why the fuck do I feel like I'm on the verge of a spontaneous orgasm?

"And no, I wasn't following you. I had a bad day and didn't

feel like going home. My parents are most likely there doing weird as fuck sex therapy shit and I'm not in the mood to see them," he explains. "Also, I know you can handle yourself. I stepped in for that dude's protection, not yours. I did it for my own sanity, too. I was afraid you'd break a nail on his face and then I'd have to listen to you bitch and moan all night long about your manicure.

I stare at him for a few minutes to see if he's telling the truth. When his gaze on me doesn't waver, I sigh loudly. "Well, I wasn't on a date. My mom pissed me off so I packed a bag and went to stay with Gavin and Charlotte. They were most likely getting ready to do some weird as fuck sex shit and I didn't feel like sticking around while Gavin licks my sister's ass."

Tyler laughs, resting his elbow on the bar, inching his way further between my legs until I can feel the material of his jeans rubbing against my inner thighs.

"What did your mom do to piss you off?"

And just like that, I open up to Tyler, the one person I never thought I would let my guard down around. I tell him about my fashion blog and how my mom shit all over my excitement with it. I tell him how much I hate working at Seduction and Snacks and how I hate where my life is going. He orders both of us another couple rounds of drinks without ever taking his eyes off of me, hanging on my every word and interjecting with little pieces of advice every now and then.

Before long, I'm buzzed and everything he says makes me laugh. My hands rest casually against his chest as he tells me about meeting his real father and something inside of me shifts. It happens so suddenly that I have to catch my breath. My heart speeds up and my hands start to sweat as I feel Tyler's heart beating under my palms. It takes me a minute to realize I'm not having a fucking heart attack. What I'm having is a moment of clarity – Tyler Branson is genuinely a nice guy. A nice guy with a huge penis, a six pack and eyes so blue they look like someone took a blue crayon and colored them in.

He's immature at times, a complete smart-ass and into some kinky shit, but he's nice to me no matter how much of a bitch I am to him; no matter how hard I try to push him away.

Son of a mother fucking bitch, I think I'm falling for Tyler.

CHAPTER 12

Hot and Juicy Wiener

- Tyler -

"Oh, yeah, that's it. Right there! A little more to the left. Lick my Christmas ornaments."

Ava's mouth stills on my dick and she looks up at me. If my penis wasn't stuffed in her mouth, I have a feeling she'd be yelling at me for something. Her mouth is so warm and wet that I really couldn't care less what she yells at me about right now. She's giving me a blow job in the women's bathroom of the bar and I am not about to tell her to pipe down with the attitude, especially when I feel her graze my dick with her teeth. Nope, never piss off a woman who holds your manhood and the lives of your future children in between her chompers.

She sucks me hard into her mouth and I smack my hands down on the wall of the bathroom stall we're in. As good as this feels, I need to stop her. I'd much rather be between her legs when I come and I have a feeling she's already pissed about the fact that she's kneeling on a bathroom floor right now.

Leaning forward, I slide my hands under her arms and haul her up from the floor, pressing her back against the wall and sliding my hands up her bare thighs. I stare into her eyes as my hands continue to move until they are wrapped around the soft, smooth flesh of her ass.

"Fuck, you're not wearing any underwear?" I mutter as she leans forward and slides the tip of her tongue across my bottom lip.

"I was, but I took them off a little while ago when I went to the bathroom. I slipped them in the pocket of your coat that's still hanging over the chair by the bar," she tells me.

Ava reaches her hand in between our bodies and wraps it around my dick, stroking me while I knead her ass and pull one of her legs up around my hip.

Once her leg is secure, I quickly reach into my back pocket for one of the condoms I stuck in there before I left the house. I told her a little white lie when she asked me if I followed her. Charlotte called me after Ava left her and Gavin's place and asked if I'd keep an eye on Ava and make sure she didn't get into any trouble. Even though Ava swore she'd never have sex with me again, I knew she wouldn't be able to keep that promise.

I quickly rip open the condom with my teeth. Ava takes it from me and easily rolls the thin rubber down the length of my cock. I sigh in pleasure as she lines me up and in one hard thrust, I'm fully inside of her, both of us groaning. I don't waste any time – I immediately start pounding into her, the bathroom stall shaking with the force of my thrusts.

"Take that purse off of your shoulder, it's in my way," I complain, grabbing onto the strap as I hold myself still inside of her.

She smacks my hand away and gives me a dirty look. "Are you insane? Do you have any idea how much this bag cost? I'm not putting it anywhere near that floor. People have pissed on that floor."

I slowly grind my hips against her and try reaching for the purse again. She closes her eyes and moans, but even with her eyes closed she knows what I'm doing and her hand latches onto my wrist in a death grip.

"Touch that bag and you die. A slow, painful death where I cut off your balls and make you eat them."

Her eyes are still closed and she hums in approval when I jerk against her. This time, I'm not trying to distract her with my awesome sexual moves; I'm honestly fucking afraid of her. That little jerk was a reflex when I thought about my balls being detached from my body and force-fed to me. You can make all the jokes you want about balls being delicious and loving the feel of balls in your mouth, but it's not funny at all when we're talking about *my* sweaty, hairy balls.

I make a mental note to shave my balls as soon as fucking possible before I start moving inside of her again. I'm guessing if Ava does make good on her threat, balls would go down a lot easier if they weren't covered in pubes.

Ava's hands clutch onto my hair and she starts mumbling

nonsense, telling me to move faster and harder as I bite and suck on the skin of her neck.

"Yeah, you like that? You like it when Big Papa gives you his hot and juicy wiener?" I pant, my hips hammering against her.

Her fists yank on my hair, pulling my head away from her neck so hard that I see stars.

"Ow! What the fuck?" I complain as she gives me a dirty look.

"You cannot say shit like that when we're fucking. You just can't," she warns me, letting out a low groan when I shift my hips and grind my pubic bone against her clit.

"What's wrong with a little dirty talk? I thought you'd like it."

Ava moves against me, matching me thrust for thrust and now it's my turn to groan.

"I like dirty talk. I LOVE dirty talk. What you're doing is not dirty talk. It's 'weird as fuck' talk. Repeat after me: I love fucking you, your pussy is so tight," Ava demands.

Well, damn, that was hot. I kind of wish I had a vagina right now.

Slowing down my movements, I start rolling my hips against her and do as she says.

"I love fucking you, your pussy is so tight," I tell her in a soft, low voice.

She moans her approval, so I continue.

"Your pussy is so tight, like trying to get a new My Little Pony out of the packaging. Like those fucking tight twisty ties-"

"Oh, my God, no! JESUS CHRIST" she interrupts.

I move my hand from her ass and slide it in between us, my thumb finding her clit and rubbing slow circles around it.

"Oh, God, oh, my God," she pants. "Okay, try this one: Your pussy is so wet and feels so good wrapped around my cock."

I hold myself inside of her and start moving my thumb faster against her clit.

"Your pussy is so wet and feels so good wrapped around my cock…like fucking a glass of warm water."

Ava grabs onto my ear lobe and yanks it as hard as she can, pulling my face towards her. "Stop fucking adlibbing!"

I pull out of her and then slam back inside, my thumb still working her over while she gasps and jerks her hips against me.

"I want to come inside you and then I want to fuck that tight little ass of yours," Ava mutters.

Pausing my hip thrusts, I stare at her in shock until she opens her eyes.

"When I told you I bought a butt plug, I didn't really think you'd take that to mean I wanted you to fuck me in the ass. Honestly, I don't even know how that works," I admit.

She rolls her eyes, moving her hands to my hips and forcing me to start pounding into her again.

"Hello? I'm giving you dirty talk suggestions. You're supposed to say that to me," she complains.

Once again, I completely stop moving.

"Wait, you want me to come inside you AND fuck your ass? You didn't talk to me for a week when I just put the tip in. I'm so confused right now," I tell her with a shake of my head.

"You know what? How about we just don't talk. At all. Just keep doing what you're doing with your thumb because I'm about two seconds away from coming," she moans.

Alrighty, that I can do.

Getting back to business, I keep my mouth shut and continue pounding into Ava, moving my thumb over her in tiny circles. Within seconds, she's screaming my name and I quickly follow right behind her. Who knew having sex in a bar bathroom could be so hot?

After we catch our breath, I pull out of her and dispose of the condom. Ava straightens her clothes and runs a hand through her long hair before we unlock the stall door and make our way back out to the bar.

"So, does this mean we can renegotiate the whole anal thing? Because I've been studying up with porn and I think I know what I did wrong last time," I tell her as we get to our seats.

"Shut up, Tyler," Ava replies.

My balls are still intact and we managed to spend a few hours together without killing one another.

I'd say this is progress.

CHAPTER 13
Wood Chipper
~ Ava ~

"Jesus Christ, these women are insipid fools who should just wear signs on their foreheads that say 'I'm a whore'," I mutter to myself.

Yes, I'm talking out loud to myself while watching *The Bachelor*. I can't help it. Even though these bitches make me want to throw myself off of a bridge, I continue to watch it. Ever since Aunt Jenny spruced up my blog, I've started writing little commentaries while I watch the show and I've noticed they get a ton of hits. Sure, I'm not talking about fashion on my fashion blog right now, but I'll do anything just to get people to click on the site.

Pulling up the app on my phone for my blog, I type up a quick post about tonight's show, letting everyone place bets on how long it will take for the first woman to start crying. The winner will get an open-knit eternity scarf from Urban Outfitters. One of the perks of having a fashion blog that's growing in popularity – designers will send me samples to try as long as I blog about them.

Social media is a crazy, awesome thing. The more I started posting on my blog, the more people started sharing my posts on Twitter, Facebook and Instagram. Pretty soon, companies got word of what I was doing and started contacting me about sending out some free stuff. Who was I to turn down free shit, especially clothes, purses and jewelry?

"Um, Ava? Could you come here for a minute?" Tyler shouts from down the hall.

Tyler has been crashing on Charlotte and Gavin's couch for the last couple of nights. After the night in the bar, I should be mad at him, but I couldn't bring myself to feel anything other than just a tiny bit happy. I knew he was lying when he said he hadn't followed me there. Charlotte told me that she let Tyler know I was going to a bar and most likely going to pick up some random dude to wash all of my sorrows away. Even though I don't do relationships, it was kind of nice to have him get a little jealous and come after me. I've never had a guy give a rat's ass about anything I do, mostly because the feeling is mutual. No guy has ever sparked my interest for longer than one night. Now that we're both living under the same roof, I'm sure whatever misguided feelings I have for him will be punched right in the face very quickly. There's no way we'll make it more than a week without killing each other.

"Ava? Are you out there?" Tyler yells again.

Case in point. I'm really fucking busy right now and he probably just wants sex.

"*The Bachelor* is on, can't it wait an hour?" I shout back.

Just then, one of the women on the show starts sobbing because she only got five minutes of alone time with that jackass they're fighting over like rabid women at a Hermes Birkin bag sample sale and now she's certain he'll never love her.

"Oh, my God, YOU JUST MET HIM!" I scream at the television.

I check my watch and realize that we have our first crier at exactly twelve minutes and seventeen seconds. Scrolling through the comments on my blog, I see that I have a winner who guessed twelve minutes correctly. Looks like she's getting a lovely scarf to commemorate the downfall of smart, independent women everywhere.

"Seriously, Ava, this can't wait!" I hear Tyler yell again.

With a roll of my eyes, I pause the DVR and toss my phone onto the couch cushions before getting up and heading down the hall.

Tyler meets me right outside the bathroom door with a towel wrapped around his hips while he chews on his bottom lip nervously.

It takes me a minute to compose myself when I see little droplets of water sliding down his chest. Thoughts of every single cheesy romance novel I've ever read float through my mind as I stand here like an idiot with my mouth open and stare at him, trying not to say things like "rock hard abs," "delicious six-pack" and anything with the words "manly" and "bulge".

Thank God Charlotte and Gavin went out for the evening. Now that I've fallen off the No Sex With Tyler Wagon, I plan on shifting that baby into high gear and riding him into the sunset.

"So, I need to show you something, but you have to promise not to laugh," Tyler says, pulling me out of my daze.

Before I can confirm or deny said promise of laughter, he yanks the towel away from his hips and drops it to the floor by his feet.

I didn't think it was possible for my mouth to open any wider than it already was. I've seen Tyler's penis before; I've had Tyler's penis in my mouth. While it's a pretty amazing sight to behold, for once that's not what has me in such a state of shock.

"Do you have a Band-Aid on your balls?" I ask incredulously as I tilt my head to the side to get a better look.

He's grabbed onto his penis at this point and pulled it up flush with his stomach so I can see what's going on. Sure enough, the area between his balls and his shaft is covered with a pink, My Little Pony Band-Aid.

"Yep, that's a Band-Aid. I sort of had an accident with the hair clippers I found under the sink in Gavin's bathroom," he admits, craning his neck to stare down at his own junk.

"You used Gavin's hair clippers to trim your ball hair? Are you insane?" I question, kneeling down to get a better look.

I should be walking away and not entertaining his odd behavior but really, how often do you get to see a dude with a Band-Aid on his balls?

"Under different circumstances, having you on your knees with your face by my cock would be so totally awesome," Tyler sighs.

I look up at him from the floor and scowl.

"But yeah, those clippers must have been from the 1950's or some shit. They sucked my pube hair into them like a fucking wood chipper and wouldn't let go. I can't believe you didn't hear me screaming from the shower. There was so much blood. Blood from my balls was everywhere. It was like Texas Chainsaw Ball Massacre."

He reaches down and starts peeling away the edge of the Band-Aid. I quickly jump up and move away, my back slamming into the wall in the narrow hallway.

"Oh, my God, what are you doing? Don't take that thing off! You're going to get your ball sack blood all over Charlotte's carpet!"

He ignores me, pulling the Band-Aid completely off and I cringe when I see the cut that goes straight up the underside of his penis. It looks like he tried to filet his junk like a fish.

"Why in the hell would you do that to yourself?" I question, shuddering when he taps his finger against the cut and then checks his finger for traces of blood.

"I just thought a little manscaping was in order. You're considerate enough to get waxed so I don't yack up a pube when I'm down there, thought I'd return the favor," he tells me with a smile.

Is it weird that I think this is kind of sweet? It's totally weird. I've lost my fucking mind.

"It's almost done bleeding," he continues, grabbing the towel from the floor and wrapping it back around his hips. "Man, I screamed like a bitch when the soap got on it in the shower. So, are we having sex tonight or what?"

Shaking my head, I turn and head back into the living room. "If getting soap on it hurt that bad, what the hell do you think my vagina is going to do to it?"

Tyler follows behind me. "Your vagina is sweet and kind and would never hurt my penis. Don't worry; it will be fine. It's way down at the bottom, so unless your vagina decides to suck up my balls, it will be okay. The bleeding should stop soon."

I turn around to face him when I get to the living room, crossing my arms in front of me. I can't help but stare back down at his crotch and feel a little sad that he covered it up. It really is a nice penis, even with a sliced scrotum.

"I am not earning my red wings with you tonight. Thanks, but no thanks," I tell him.

"Hey, I earned my red wings with YOU. It's only fair you reciprocate," he argues.

"That was an accident! You banged my period right out of me." Tyler laughs and puffs out his chest. "Yeah, I did. I should get that on a t-shirt. 'This guy bangs out Aunt Flo'."

He may be annoying, but he's phenomenal in bed. I have to clench my thighs together just thinking about how many orgasms he'll give me tonight.

"Fine, but if you get blood on Charlotte's sheets, you're explaining it to her," I warn him.

CHAPTER 14

Hoity Toity

- Tyler -

I inhale deeply and settle back into the couch next to Gavin just as Ava walks in from the kitchen with a glass of water in her hand.

"Did you just smell your fingers?" she asks me in horror.

Gavin and Charlotte got home from dinner as I stripped the condom off of my dick, leaving Ava in the bed blessedly silent after orgasm number four. You'll be happy to know there was no blood shed. Actually, Charlotte will be happy to know that since she does the laundry and won't have to worry about getting scrotum blood out of sheets.

I wiggle my fingers in the air at her and smile. "Yes, I did just smell my fingers, thank you for asking."

She looks at me in revulsion. "Why? Why would you do that?"

Gavin and I look at each other and shrug, speaking at the same time. "It's a guy thing."

Ava looks like she's going to puke. She mutters something about us being gross before heading down the hall to return to bed.

"I don't understand why women don't get that? You would think it's a compliment that I want to carry around her smell with me forever," I complain.

Gavin nods his head in sympathy.

"So, you haven't said a word about meeting your dad the other day. I know I kind of made fun of the fact that his parents hated him for giving him such a shitty name, but other than that, how was it?" he asks.

I let out a big sigh, the smell of my fingers forgotten for the moment. "Dude, I don't get it. I mean, my mom had to go through profiles to pick out the sperm she wanted. Out of every sperm in the book, that's who she picked?"

"Well, it's not like she was looking for a father figure, just a donor. Who cares if you guys have nothing in common," Gavin states.

"Um, nothing in common would be an understatement. The guy asked our waitress for crayons during dessert and then ate the blue ones because he said they taste like purple. I had to keep all of the napkins away from him because he tried to eat those, too, and when the bill came he asked if he could pay for it with red Skittles. It was like eating lunch with a toddler."

Gavin raises his eyebrow at me. "So, you're saying he was really immature? Wow, that doesn't sound anything like you."

I punch him in the arm and scowl at him. "I will have you know, I'm a fun, enthusiastic immature. This guy was just fucking weird."

"Did you talk to your mom about it?" Gavin asks.

I don't even want to think about my mom right now. When I went to the house to pack a bag and tell her I needed some time away to get my thoughts in order, she gave me a book on Kama Sutra and told me some new sex moves might cheer me up. I tested out the Inverted Cow and the Splitting Bamboo in the kitchen earlier and, while those did perk me up a little bit, The Deckchair and the Lustful Leg totally fucked up my thigh and now I have a pulled muscle. All I wanted from her was an explanation as to why she never told me the truth. All of those fucking sex ed homeschooling classes she made me sit through and she never once thought it would be a great idea to tell me she picked up some strange spunk at a drive-thru window?

"I'm done talking to my mom. Her answer to everything is sex," I complain.

"Um, your answer to everything is sex," Gavin reminds me.

"Well, yeah, but it's just gross when it's my mom suggesting it."

Gavin leans back into the cushions and we both kick our legs up on the coffee table. "Did you ever think that maybe the sperm bank made a mistake? I mean, I don't want to get your hopes up or anything, but I'm sure that sort of thing happens from time to time. Maybe they just pulled the wrong record or something."

That very thought crossed my mind right about the time Dean O'Saur started eating butter packets with a knife and fork without removing the foil wrapper.

"What if I find out that the sperm she used isn't even what got her pregnant? My mom told me herself she was kind of a slut and had a foursome the same week she went to the sperm back. God only knows who my father could be. Jesus God, what if it's someone worse than Dean O'Saur?"

Gavin laughs. "I don't think there is anyone worse than Dean O'Saur, unless he has a brother named Terry Dactyl."

"Actually, that's not a bad name. That would make me Tyler Dactyl. That's kind of bad ass," I consider.

"It doesn't have to be someone worse, you know. What if it's someone totally awesome? A rich, Hollywood actor or something. You could be a millionaire and not even know it."

The more I think about this, the more excited I get. "Oh, my God, what if my dad is Peter New?"

Gavin stares at me in confusion.

"Um, hello? Peter New? The voice actor for Big Macintosh on My Little Pony? God, it's like you live in a cave or something," I complain.

"I was thinking more along the lines of Brad Pitt or Robert Downey, Jr."

Now it's my turn to look at him like he's crazy. "Who?"

Gavin shakes his head at me and I ignore him. This idea has already taken root inside my brain and it totally makes sense. I mean, Peter New is from Canada, which is like right by Ohio. I think. I could see him hanging out on college campuses and hooking up with my mom. I mean, I can't actually see *that* part or else I'd have to pour bleach in my eyes, but it has to be true.

"Even if it's not Peter New, it could definitely be Trevor Devall," I think aloud. "I mean, he's an older dude but my mom wouldn't care about that. She's an equal opportunity banger."

When Gavin doesn't reply, I turn my head to see he still has a blank look on his face.

"God, you are so out of the loop it's scary. Trevor Devall is the voice of Hoity Toity. Not one of my favorites, but still a great character in his own right. He always makes good choices, he's an Earth Pony and a major representative of the fashion world. Which would totally explain my attraction to Ava."

"Alright, slow your roll there, Pinkie Pie," Gavin interrupts. "I'm pretty sure your dad isn't going to be someone who does voices for My Little Pony."

"For your information, Pinkie Pie is a chick. It's not biologically possible for a chick to be my dad, nice try. And hello? You thought my dad could be Robert Pitt or Brad Downey, Jr. or whatever," I fire back."

"That's not...you know what? You're right," Gavin says, throwing his hands up in the in defeat. "Your dad could technically be anyone and you won't know for sure unless you contact the sperm back."

"I already contacted them."

"HOLY SHIT!" Gavin and I shout in surprise at the same time as we turn to see Molly standing at the end of the couch staring down at her cell phone.

"Where the fuck did you come from? How long have you been here?" I demand.

She just shrugs without taking her eyes off of her phone. "I've been here all night."

"Uh, all night?"

Molly finally looks up with a blank expression on her face. I swear to God she's a fucking robot or cyborg or some shit.

"Yes, all night. I was here for the wood chipper incident and listened to you cry about a My Little Pony butt plug. You know I'm only nineteen, right? I'm in the prime of my youth and you just scarred me for life."

Gavin turns away from Molly to look at me. "Wood chipper?"

I shake my head at him. "That's for another time, my friend."

Looking back at Molly, I get back to the important matter at hand. "You said you contacted them. Who did you contact?"

She rolls her eyes at me and if I wasn't afraid that she's a secret agent with the CIA and probably knows a hundred different ways to decapitate a man, I'd probably get lippy with her.

"I emailed the sperm back while you two Nancys were learning a new Friendship is Magic secret handshake," she deadpans.

"There's a secret handshake?" Gavin asks.

"NO! Ponies don't have hands! And the MLP's wouldn't reduce themselves to such trivial group activities," I inform them with disgust.

"Anyway," Molly continues. "They emailed me right back and apologized for the mix-up. Turns out you were right. Dean O'Saur isn't your real dad. They've been converting all of their old paper files to a new system and got your mom's information switched with someone else's. You have a meeting with them tomorrow at noon."

And with that, Molly shoves her phone in her back pocket and heads out the front door.

"Well, the good news is, you don't have to worry about sharing a meal of Crayolas at Dean's house for the holidays. The bad news is, when I marry Charlotte, I'll be related to Molly and I'll always have to sleep with one eye open," Gavin says with a sigh.

Looks like it's back to the drawing board for me. Fingers crossed that the sperm bank gets it right this time. Otherwise, I'm heading to BronyCon and finding my dad on my own.

CHAPTER 15
Stripper Glitter
~ Ava ~

"No, no, no, you're doing it wrong. The Santa heads have to have blue eyes. Oh, my God, just let me do it."

Aunt Jenny, Charlotte, my mom and I all put down our knives and slowly back away from the table as Aunt Claire curses and scowls at us.

She invites us over every year to help her decorate the cookies for Christmas day, and every year she bitches at us for doing it wrong.

"For the love of God, slutbag, it doesn't matter if Santa has blue eyes or green eyes," my mom complains.

We all watch as Aunt Claire stalks towards her, waving a butter knife dripping with red frosting that looks a hell of a lot like blood.

"I don't tell you how to diddle yourself with vibrators, you don't tell me how to decorate my cookies, fuck face!"

Before this gets out of hand and frosting starts flying around the kitchen, Charlotte and I separate the two of them. Aunt Claire goes back to making her cookies perfect while my mom makes everyone some coffee.

For right now, the two of us have called a truce. I'm not ready to move back home yet and she's not ready to accept the fact that I don't want to spend my days filing order forms for Pocket Pussies, but at least she's stopped making snarky comments about my blog for the moment.

"So, any news on when my son is going to propose?" Aunt Claire asks nonchalantly.

I watch as Charlotte's face reddens in embarrassment and I can't help but be a little happy that she's in the hot seat for once instead of me.

"Um, I don't…uh, oh, my God," Charlotte stammers, looking at me with wide eyes and a look on her face that clearly says "Help me the fuck out".

I just shrug and smile at her. I'd like to know the answer to this question, as well. The two of them are already acting like they're married; they might as well make it official.

"I bet he'll do it on Christmas in front of everyone," I offer.

Charlotte shoots me a dirty look and I can't help but laugh. We've talked plenty of times over the years about the perfect proposal and Charlotte hates the idea of it going down on a holiday in front of a bunch of people. Especially people as insane as our family.

"Oh, thank God. If your Aunt Claire doesn't get to wear that blue dress she bought for the wedding soon, her ass is going to outgrow it," mom says as she pours herself a cup of coffee.

"Well, at least my tits won't be falling out of my dress like a cheap hooker," Aunt Claire adds, not looking up from her frosting work.

"Hey, I am a high priced hooker, get it right," mom fires back.

"I love you, bitch," Aunt Claire says with a smile.

Mom puts her hand over her heart. "Right back at you, skank."

Right then, Aunt Jenny burst into tears.

"What the hell, Jenny? You know we love you too," mom says in confusion, walking up behind her and patting her on the back.

Charlotte grabs a few tissues from the box on the counter and holds them out for Aunt Jenny to take. She blows her nose and takes a few minutes to calm down before she speaks.

"I think Drew is cheating on me," she tells us with a sniffle.

"I will cut off his dick and shove it down his throat," my mom states angrily.

Aunt Claire puts her frosting knife down and holds up her hands. "Wait just a minute. Why in the hell would you think Drew is cheating on you?"

"When we had sex the other night, he said he was too tired to use the nipple clamps and chip dip," Aunt Jenny complains, starting to cry again.

"Oh, gross. You two are almost fifty. Is there ever going to come a time when you have sex like normal people?" mom complains.

Ignoring her, Aunt Claire continues with her questions. "So, aside from that, is there anything else? I mean, maybe he really was just tired."

Aunt Jenny dabs at her eyes with a tissue. "He's been gone a lot lately and he keeps telling me he has meetings, but I think he's lying. Three times in the last week, I've found glitter on his clothes."

"He's probably just going to a strip club or something," Charlotte tells her with a shrug.

Aunt Jenny shakes her head. "No, it's definitely not stripper glitter. This glitter was thick and dark. Stripper glitter is fine and antidepressant."

"Well, I've always wondered if stripper glitter had anxiety issues," my mom mutters.

"Do you mean iridescent?" Charlotte asks Aunt Jenny softly.

"I don't know. I don't know anything anymore," Aunt Jenny sighs. "Just forget about it. I'm going to sit Drew down and make him tell me what's going on. I swear to God if he's having sex with another woman and didn't ask me to join, beds are gonna roll."

Mom groans. "HEADS are gonna roll, Jenny, HEADS."

"Okay, change of subject," Aunt Claire announces, turning to look at Charlotte. "I'm going to make a 'Congratulations on your Engagement' cake for you and Gavin to serve at Christmas dinner, so let me know what flavor you want. Oh, and your mom and I already picked out the invitations for the engagement party and I've got some great new cookie cutters of diamond rings we can use for favors-"

"Ava is falling for Tyler!" Charlotte suddenly shouts, cutting off Aunt Claire.

"What the fuck, Charlotte?" I yell back.

I get that she's freaking out about the prospect of getting engaged and everyone planning everything before it's even happened, but Jesus, she didn't need to throw me under the damn bus! Falling for Tyler…as if!

"Well, as luck would have it, we just got a new line of My Little Pony sex toys in at the shop," mom says with a sigh. "You'll never run out of gifts to celebrate your love. I'm particularly fond of the My Little Pony Fleshlight. They come in pretty colors."

Aunt Jenny finally perks up after her little meltdown. "I bought Drew one of those already! I also got him the Lyra Plushie and he can stick his penis in her ass. She's so cute. But word to the wide, make sure Tyler doesn't finish in her. Whatever she's made out of is a bitch to clean."

We all groan in disgust.

"I am not falling for Tyler and I will not be supporting his freaky My Little Pony habit by purchasing anything from that line of toys, thank you very much," I inform them.

Just because he has fabulous abs and a perfect dick, he's easy to talk to and occasionally says really nice things to me doesn't mean I'm falling in love with him. That's just stupid.

"Did you hear about what happened with the whole sperm bank mix up?" Charlotte asks.

Everyone nods and mutters words of compassion for Tyler

while I stand there in confusion for several minutes until Charlotte notices.

"He didn't tell you? Dude, the sperm bank fucked up their records and gave him the wrong name. Now they can't figure out where his mom's records are so he has no idea who his dad is all over again. He's been really down about it," Charlotte explains.

What? Why didn't he tell me this?

I've been so busy worrying about my own problems that it didn't even occur to me to ask Tyler about his. I suck.

Wait, what? No, I don't suck. Who cares about his problems? He's a booty call, nothing more.

But shit, he must feel awful. I couldn't even imagine what it would be like to not know who my dad is. I don't like all of these conflicting feelings that are going on inside of me right now. All of a sudden I feel like doing something nice for him. I don't do nice. What the hell is wrong with me?

Shit, there is no way I'm falling for Tyler Branson.

CHAPTER 16

Pulsating Posey

- Tyler -

"We need to talk."

I quickly remove my hand from the My Little Pony butt plug I may or may not have been petting and turn around to face Ava.

"Does that sex toy have a pink horse tail on it?" she questions, tilting her head to the side to look around me.

"I wasn't touching it!"

She rights her head and raises her eyebrow.

"Ok, fine. I was touching it, but it's so soft and silky," I admit.

Ava shakes her head like she's trying to clear all thoughts of me playing with a butt plug with an attached tail.

"Anyway, I think we should talk," she tries again.

I don't like how serious she looks. Ava and I don't do serious. We do sex and we snap at each other and we do both quite well.

This can only mean one thing – she doesn't want us doing the sex anymore.

Fuck.

"Can we go somewhere else? I feel dirty standing in an aisle of My Little Pony sex toys. Holy shit, does that vibrator have a My Little Pony head on it?" she asks in awe, stepping around me and reaching for the yellow and pink vibrator in the box next to the MLP Fleshlights.

"That's Pulsating Posey. On the show she's known for her garden of flowers. At Seduction and Snacks, she's known for titillating the petals of the flower between your legs," I explain.

She quickly tosses Pulsating Posey back into the box, turning back around to face me. If I'm not mistaken, I think PP might have turned Ava on just a little bit. If this chick suddenly develops a fondness for all things MLP, I'm going to have a hard time walking away from her.

"So, you want to talk, huh?" I ask her with a sigh. "Come on, let's go into my office."

I turn and walk down the aisle like a man going to the electric chair. I guess I should have known this was coming. Someone as beautiful and confident as Ava doesn't hang around a guy like me for that long. Sure, I have a better job and I'm not living in my parent's basement anymore, but I'm not exactly at the top of the "Great Catch" list either.

In the front corner of the warehouse, they've set up a small room for me to use as an office. It used to be a storage room and it doesn't have any windows, but it has a desk, a filing cabinet, a door that locks and a computer so I can watch porn in peace during my lunch hour. When we get inside, I close the door behind Ava and wait for her to drop the ax and bring an end to our magical time together of fucking like rabbits.

Ava perches her hip on the edge of my desk and I lean against the closed door with my arms crossed in front of me. I've had plenty of fantasies about screwing her on top of that desk and I'm a little sad that I won't get to fulfill them. Unless, of course, she's down with one last go for old time's sake.

"We've been spending a lot of time together and I realized that all we do is have sex," Ava starts, wringing her hands in her lap and cracking her knuckles nervously. "It's nice and all, but I thought we should talk. You know, try something new."

I can't stop the laugh that bursts out of my mouth. "Talk? You actually want to act like a nice human being?"

She winces, quickly looking back down at her hands and I immediately want to take my words back. I know we constantly bicker back and forth and can lob insults at each other with the best of them, but I can tell something is different with her this time. Here I was lamenting the fact that I'd never get to have sex with her again while she wanted to do something normal like talk and I go and fuck it up with my mouth.

"I didn't mean-"

Ava holds up her hand and cuts me off. "No, I get it, I'm a bitch."

"You're not a bitch."

She cocks her head and looks at me like I'm an idiot.

"Okay fine, you're a little bit of a bitch, but I don't care and obviously it turns me on," I admit, pushing away from the door and walking closer to her.

"I know I act like I don't care and that I'm just sticking around for the sex. I'm not used to someone like you. I've never been with anyone who I could tolerate for more than a day or two. I never expected for...*this*," she gestures between us. "To amount to anything. I never expected to *feel* things. I certainly never expected to be hurt when I found out something happened with your bio-dad situation and you didn't tell me yourself."

She lets out an uneasy laugh and I move even closer, sliding my body in between her legs and resting my hands on her hips. The only sides of Ava I've ever seen are sexy- hot and annoyed-bitchy. I didn't think it was possible to want her more than I already did, but I was wrong. Seeing her vulnerable and nervous as she opens up to me just the tiniest bit makes me want to rip all of her clothes off and make her mine.

"I think it's probably obvious to everyone that I'm unhappy with my life and where it's going. I took it out on you and I'm sorry about that," she says softly.

"You don't have to apologize. You drive me crazy, but I have more fun fighting with you than I've ever had getting along with anyone else," I explain, bring a hand up to the side of her face and cupping her cheek in my palm. "I have a My Little Pony fetish and I don't know any woman who would put up with that shit, but you sort of do and I like that about you."

She smiles at me and like a fucking chick, my heart skips a beat.

I'm pretty sure I've never seen Ava smile unless she was plotting something evil and calculating. This smile is soft and lights up her entire face.

Yep, it's happened, folks. I've grown a vagina.

"Why are you so unhappy with your life? You've got a great job, the perfect family and you get boned by a dude with mad bedroom skills on a regular basis," I smirk.

Ava laughs and shakes her head at me, sliding her hands around my waist. "I do have a good job, but it's not the job I want. It doesn't make me happy."

I move my fingers under her chin and force her to look up at me. "What do you want, Ava? What makes you happy?"

She bites her lip before taking a deep breath and spilling everything to me. She tells me about her blog and how her mom is always putting it down. She uses words like "couture" and "fashion forecast" that I've never even heard of before. She gets more and more excited and animated as she talks and I can't help but smile. I've never seen her so passionate about something before and it makes me angry that her mom doesn't at least try to understand.

For the first time in my life, a chick is talking to me and I'm not zoning out and imagining what she would look like wearing only a unicorn headband.

Okay, fine. I lost concentration for a second when she mentioned "trunk show." Come on. What guy hears *trunk* and doesn't immediately think *ass?* For the most part, though, I'm right here with her, hanging on her every word. I want to see her happy like this all the time. I don't know what this blog thing entails, but

I'm going to help her. If I can start a Bronies Support group in Ohio with only five members, my parents' garage, two VCR's and a poor, lost soul who was still in love with Rainbow Brite, then by God I will make this happen for her.

Even though Ava said all we did was have sex and she wanted to spend some time talking, we were alone in my locked office and I had a Pulsating Posey in my top desk drawer.

After our talk, I may have convinced Ava of the appeal of My Little Pony.

Three times.

CHAPTER 17
Genital Flogging
~ Ava ~

"You'll never guess who I just got off the phone with-"

I stop abruptly in Charlotte and Gavin's living room when I see Tyler on the couch with a book in his hands.

"Are you reading an erotic romance book?" I ask in shock after I got a peek at the cover.

Sticking an old receipt in between the pages to mark his place, Tyler sets the book down on the coffee table and looks up at me.

"Well, I heard this stuff is all the rage with the ladies so I thought I'd give it a go. I've decided that you should start calling me Master."

I roll my eyes and plop down on the couch next to him. "That's never going to happen."

I was a little worried moving in with Gavin and Charlotte that

I'd never have any time to myself. Now that Tyler and I are sort of a *thing*, I figured we'd never get any alone time together either, but it's actually worked out in our favor. The two of them are never home. They're either working or going out together.

"It says in that book that women like to be dominated, so I think you should submit to me," Tyler states.

"Um, have you met me? I'm not like those women. There is no way I would let you walk all over me."

Tyler turns to face me on the couch. "Come on, be adventurous. I'll tie you to the bed and spank you. We just need a safe word," he muses.

"I've got a safe word. If you ever spank me and I scream 'DON'T FUCKING SPANK ME AGAIN', that's my cue for you to stop."

Tyler looks at me funny. "That's a really long safe word. I was thinking more along the lines of 'nipple' or 'pancakes'. Something simple."

"Tyler, focus! Stop thinking about BDSM for five minutes. I just got off the phone with Nordstrom's and they want to buy ad space on my blog."

After our talk the other day in Tyler's office, he asked me how many hits I got on my blog each time I post. When I told him the number, his mouth dropped open in surprise and he told me with numbers like that, I could definitely get a few sponsors that would pay me for advertising. I didn't think he was serious until he started making phone calls for me and the companies actually called me back. With this recent call from Nordstrom's, I now have five businesses paying me a monthly fee for advertising.

"See? I told you that you'd be able to make money off of this thing," he tells me with a smile. "Let's celebrate with some light bondage and role-playing."

I shake my head at him, grab his hand and pull him up from the couch. "I've got a better idea. I need to do a blog post today about a few of the items Charlotte Russe and Forever 21 sent me over the weekend and I need a model."

Tyler stops in the middle of the room and refuses to let me continue pulling him towards the bedroom. "Whoa, hold up there, missy. I don't know if I'm comfortable with this."

Putting on my best pouting face, I bat my eyelashes at him. "But they sent over a My Little Pony t-shirt. If you put it on and let me take a picture of you in it, I promise we can try out the whole bondage thing."

Tyler narrows his eyes. "Is this t-shirt bedazzled?"

"It's bedazzled AND it came with a multi-colored tail that attaches to the belt loop of your pants," I tell him.

Tyler grabs my hand this time and races towards the bedroom. "Damn woman! Next time, lead with that!"

"Ooooh that tickles, do it again!"

Smack.

"Okay, that one stung a little, not so hard."

Smack.

"FUCKING HELL THAT HURT! NOT SO HARD!"

Smack, smack!

"OH, MY GOD! I SAID NOT SO HARD!"

"Safe word, use the fucking safe word!"

"PANCAKES, PANCAKES, MOTHER FUCKING PANCAKES!" Tyler screams.

With a sigh, I drop the horsetail that came with the My Little Pony t-shirt and smile at his red ass. "You were right, this bondage stuff is fun."

Tyler looks over his shoulder at me and scowls. "Can you untie me now? It would be really awkward if Charlotte and Gavin come home early."

He starts to struggle against the pair of panty hose that I wrapped securely around his wrists before tying them to the curtain rod in the living room. I've got to say, seeing him trussed up to the window buck naked with his arms above his head is kind of a nice sight and it almost pains me to untie him.

"Honey, I'm home!"

I jump at the sound of Gavin walking through the door. The smile dies on his face as he takes in the scene in his living room.

"Well, this is unexpected," he mutters.

"Oh, hey, Gavin! In case you were wondering, your curtain rods are pretty sturdy," Tyler informs him.

"Things that can never be unseen," Gavin mumbles, unable to take his eyes off of Tyler.

"So, funny story. Tyler was helping me model some clothes for my blog, one thing led to another and we decided to try out some BDSM. You're lucky you got here when you did. Cock and ball torture was next on the list," I explain.

"Wait, what?" Tyler asks in horror, craning his neck even more to look at me.

"Oh, don't be such a baby. Surely Mr. We-Need-A-Safe-Word isn't afraid of a little genital flogging," I tell him, reaching up to untie his arms.

Arms free, he turns around, rubbing his wrists. "What are you doing home so early? And where's Charlotte?"

Gavin stares up at the ceiling. "Can you please put some pants on? I cannot have a conversation with you when your third leg is pointing at me."

Grabbing Tyler's jeans from the couch, I toss them at him. After he pulls them on, Gavin finally looks back down.

"Anyway, Charlotte had a meeting at work. I wanted to get home before her because I need some advice," Gavin explains, walking into the room.

He starts to sit down on the couch, but stops his descent with his ass hovering right above the cushions. "Did you guys have sex on this couch?"

Tyler shakes his head. "Nope."

Gavin drops the rest of the way, kicking his feet up on the coffee table.

"Not today at least, but we did yesterday. I think you're sitting in the wet spot."

Gavin jumps up from the couch like it's on fire and gives both of us a dirty look. "Seriously you guys? I think I liked it better when you two hated each other."

Tyler flips Gavin off and takes a seat on the love seat, pulling me down next to him and wrapping his arm around my waist.

"What kind of advice do you need? If it's about what you just witnessed here, make sure you and Charlotte are on the same page with the safe word. It's imperative for the safety of your scrotum," Tyler tells him.

"Jesus God, no. I want to propose to Charlotte and I have no idea how to do it," Gavin tells us.

I knew this was coming. I've been teasing Charlotte about it for weeks, but hearing Gavin come right out and say it is bittersweet. My sister has found the love of her life and he wants to marry her. She has her dream job, her dream man and everything is falling into place for her.

Looking over at Tyler, I see the huge grin on his face and I can't help but smile right along with him. My sister is getting married. My blog is starting to make money and I'm pretty sure I might be in love with Tyler.

"I've got the perfect proposal idea for you," Tyler tells Gavin. "We just need to find an Alpaca farm, a place that will let us use illegal fireworks and a working fountain we can add red Jell-O to."

I must be insane.

CHAPTER 18

Sparkly Penis

- Tyler -

"You haven't talked very much about the situation with your real dad. I know we're trying out this whole talking thing now, but all we seem to talk about is me," Ava says during our lunch break at work.

"I'm an open book. You already know everything. The sperm bank had a mix-up with the records and they have no fucking clue who the sperm donor was. My only hope at this point is that my mom remembers who she had the foursome with in college so I can try and contact those dudes," I explain to her.

"There's got to be something else you can do," she says, gathering up her trash and tossing it in the bin in the corner of the room.

"Oh, there is. I'm going to BronyCon to find my dad."

She turns to face me. "You're going to what?"

"Uh, hello? BronyCon, only the biggest My Little Pony convention in the entire world. They're having it in Cleveland this year the week after Christmas and I'm going."

Before I can further explain my epic plan and possibly ask her to go with me, the door to the lunch room opens and Gavin comes running in.

"I just saw Jim in the hall and I told him I was going to ask Charlotte to marry me and now I'm pretty sure he's going to kill me," Gavin says in a rush.

"I doubt Jim is not going to kill you because you want to marry his daughter," I laugh.

He ducks down behind my chair just as the door flies open again and Jim stalks in.

"Where is he? Where is that little maggot?"

Ava rushes up to her dad and throws her arms around him. "Hi, Daddy! It's so good to see you. Why don't we go find mom?"

Jim untangles her arms from around his neck and moves her to the side. "Not now, honey. I have a man to kill."

"See?!" Gavin whispers behind me.

I watch as Jim's eyes narrow when he catches sight of Gavin crouched down and rocking back and forth behind my chair.

"Dude, stand down. You aren't going to kill Gavin," Drew says, walking through the door and wrapping his hands around Jim's arms.

"Fine, I won't kill him. I just want to talk to him, loudly and with a few punches to his nut sack," Jim states quietly.

Standing up from my chair, I walk around the table to stand in front of Jim. "Mr. Gillmore, I'd just like to say that-"

"Move out of the way, fuck face, or I'll kick your ass instead," Jim interrupts.

I nod and step out of his way. "Very good, sir."

"Get your ass out from behind that chair," Jim yells to Gavin.

Ava inches towards the door. "I'm gonna go get help."

She turns and flees from the room and I have a sudden need to follow her. Jim is a scary motherfucker when he's angry and right now, he's pissed.

We watch as Gavin slowly stands up, his eyes darting all around the room, looking for a way out.

"What the hell is going on in here? Someone said there was a fight happening," Liz says as she walks into the room a few seconds later with Claire right on her heals.

"There's nothing to see here, ladies. How about you just go on back to work and let me handle this," Jim tells Liz. "Gavin and I are going to settle this like men."

Jim clenches his fists and brings them up in front of his face. "You want to marry my daughter? Then it's time for a little Fight Club."

Claire lets out a huff and puts her hands on her hips. "Oh, hell no! Fight Club is for Liz and me. You don't get to have Fight Club! The first rule of Fight Club is that you don't get to have fucking Fight Club!"

"Wait just a minute here," Liz interrupts. "Did Gavin seriously ask your permission to marry Charlotte? That is the sweetest thing I've ever heard!"

Jim sighs, never taking his eyes off of Gavin. "You're not helping. He is not marrying our daughter."

"Wouldn't you rather they get married so that the things he's currently doing to her that are illegal in ten states aren't frowned upon?" I ask.

"Boom! That just happened!" Drew shouts, holding his hand up for me to give him a high-five.

I reach up to smack it, quickly pulling my arm back down when I see Jim give me the look of death.

"Hey, is that glitter on your hand?" I ask Drew, taking a closer look at the sparkles on his palm.

Drew drops his arm and frantically tries to wipe his hand on his pants. "I'm not doing anything wrong or weird. Sometimes I like to cover my hand in glitter and then jerk off with it because it makes everything pretty like a rainbow, so you can all just shut up right now!"

Everyone stares at him, Gavin's pending beat-down momentarily forgotten.

"Even though I'm going to regret asking this, the glitter is seriously from you jerking off and not cheating on Jenny?" Liz asks.

"Cheating on Jenny? Why would I ever cheat on Jenny?" Drew asks in shock.

"Well, she thinks you're cheating on her because you keep making excuses to leave the house and you come home covered in strange glitter that she swears isn't stripper glitter," Claire informs him.

"This is craft glitter. Everyone knows stripper glitter is more miniscule, comes in brighter colors and smells like vanilla," Drew tells us with a roll of his eyes.

I grab Drew's wrist and pull his hand close to my face. There's something familiar about this glitter but I can't wrap my head around it.

"I've seen this glitter somewhere before," I mutter.

Drew snatches his hand back. "No you haven't! You have no idea what you're talking about! It's my special glitter and all it does is make my penis sparkle!"

"I think I liked this conversation much better when we were discussing all the ways Uncle Jim was going to kill me," Gavin states with a disgusted look on his face.

"Yes, let's get back to that, shall we?" Jim asks, moving to the edge of the table, opposite Gavin. "Did you knock up my daughter?"

"Oh, for the love of God," Liz complains.

"What?! No!" Gavin shouts.

Jim starts to move around the table towards Gavin. "But you've been having sex with my daughter when the rules clearly state that I only let the two of you live together as long as you didn't touch her."

Gavin shuffles the opposite way around the table.

"Charlotte is NOT pregnant, I swear. We don't even want kids! I love her and she loves me. I want to spend the rest of my life with her," Gavin tells Jim, circling the table to get away from him.

"Jim, stop trying to kill Gavin. I have a meeting I'm late for," Liz complains.

"Calm down, Jim. They're probably just having anal. Anal doesn't count," Drew announces.

Gavin laughs and Jim stops moving, glaring at him across the table.

I really feel like I should do something to stop this. Gavin is my best friend and I don't want to see him get the shit kicked out him by his future father-in-law. Glancing around the room I see that Ava never came back after getting Liz and her Aunt Claire so it's now or never.

The word-vomit starts flowing before I even think about what I'm doing. "I'm pretty sure I might be falling in love with Ava, I'm a certified Brony, I let Ava spank me with a My Little Pony tail and my safe word is pancakes."

Before I can recover my breath from my outburst, Jim's fist connects with my cheek and stars burst in front of my eyes. The next thing I know, I'm hitting the floor with a groan.

"Dude, my safe word is 'waffles.' I knew I liked you for a reason," Drew states, staring down at me.

He holds out his hand out and helps me up to my feet while I cradle one hand against my cheek that's screaming in pain.

Everyone stands around with their mouths wide open staring at Jim, waiting to see what he's going to do next. Hopefully he's not going to hit me again because Jesus fuck that hurt.

"Well, I feel better. Let's go plan this proposal," Jim states, shaking the soreness from his hand as he turns and walks out of the room.

CHAPTER 19

Interstate

~ Ava ~

I try to steady myself on the sidewalk as Charlotte turns away from me to greet her best friend Rocco, but the entire street continues to swirl in front of me and I have a feeling I'm going to tip over if I don't grab onto something.

I've been a little out of sorts since I realized I might be in love with Tyler. I told Charlotte she needed to take me out tonight so I could spend some time away from him and get my head on straight. Unfortunately, I decided to get a head start with a few people from work. By the time Charlotte pulled up to the bar in a cab to get me, my head was long gone at the bottom of a few glasses of booze.

"Why is your sister sprawled on top of a stack of chairs?" I hear Rocco ask as the two of them walk towards me.

I lift my head and yep, I found a nice, comfy stack of chairs right outside the restaurant to lean against.

"I can't stand. Someone fucked up the sidewalk and it's all uneven," I complain as Charlotte grabs one of my arms and Rocco grabs the other, pulling me off of the chairs.

Rocco looks down at the ground and then back up at me. "Sweetie, why are you only wearing one shoe?"

I quickly look down and notice he's right. No wonder I can't walk. Why the hell do I only have on one shoe?

"I lost a shoe. Son of a fuck, I LOST A SHOE!"

I'm screaming. I know I'm screaming and there's nothing I can do about it.

Charlotte and Rocco hold onto me as they both examine my feet.

"How the hell did you lose a shoe?" Charlotte asks as I lift into the air a foot that's missing one nude Lauren Conrad platform heel, wiggling my naked toes.

"THAT FUCKING CAB STOLE MY LC SHOE! FUCK YOU CAB!" I shout, shaking my fist in the air at the cab that pulled away ten minutes ago.

Charlotte pushes me into Rocco and tells him to keep an eye on me for a minute as she runs inside a corner store next to the restaurant.

"You're really cute, Rocco. We should make out," I tell him, trying not to slur as I rest my head on his chest and he wraps his arms around me.

Rocco is a great guy and even though he's one of Charlotte's best friends, he's quickly become my friend, too. He endeared himself further when he pretended to be Charlotte's boyfriend a few months ago to make Gavin jealous. I wonder why Charlotte never dated him?

"You're really drunk, and I'm still gay," he reminds me.

Oh, that's right, he's gay.

"Plus, your sister already informed me that you're in love with Tyler. Is that why you're a hot mess tonight?" he continues.

I push away from him and put my hands on my hips. "I am NOT a hot mess, I'm FABULOUS!"

Rocco looks me over from head to toe. "Ghetto fabulous, maybe. You're wearing one shoe and that black eyeliner is staging a protest as it runs down your face in fear."

He puts his hands on either side of my face and uses his thumbs to swipe away the mess under my eyes.

"You know, there's nothing wrong with being in love with Tyler," he tells me softly. Before I can argue with him, Charlotte comes back outside with a bag in her hand. "Alright, dumbass, I got you a pair of shoes. Give me your foot."

Rocco holds me tighter as I let Charlotte remove my one, lonely shoe and replace it with a pair of flats. I'm too drunk to care that I'm letting a cheap pair of shoes from a corner store touch my feet.

"Alright, let's go get some food in you to sop up some of that alcohol," Charlotte announces as we make our way into the restaurant.

After we've been seated and our orders taken, Charlotte and Rocco sit across from me silently, waiting for me to start talking.

I don't want to talk. I don't want to think about the fact that

I'm so totally in love with Tyler that I want to cry. I just want to drink more and forget all about it.

"WHOSE FUCKING SHOES ARE THESE?" I yell, staring down at the ugly black and white slip-on flats.

Charlotte shakes her head at me. "Dude, I just bought you those at the store, remember?"

Whatever, she's totally lying. Someone stole my shoes and replaced them with these monstrosities.

"So, let's talk. Why are you so afraid of falling in love?" Rocco asks, taking a sip of his wine.

I lean forward, smacking my hands down on the table so hard the glasses and plates clink together. "I am NOT afraid of falling in love! I love falling in love. Falling in love is lovely and I *love* love."

"She's never been in love before, that's her problem," Charlotte pipes up.

"I have too been in love before!" I argue.

She cocks her head at me. "Name one time."

I'd close my eyes and try to think but I'm afraid the room will swirl too fast and I'll fall out of my chair. After a few seconds, I snap my fingers excitedly.

"Two years ago, March 17th. It was a Monday and the time was exactly 8:54 pm. I fell in love so hard that it took my breath away. It was so hard and so good. Mmmmmm, hard and good and big and I felt so full…of love and stuff," I slur.

"I'm very uncomfortable with this conversation right now," Rocco mumbles.

"Didn't you get your first Michael Kors bag two years ago?"

Charlotte questions suspiciously.

I shrug, slumping back in my chair as the waiter comes over to the table and begins setting plates of food down in front of us.

"Michael Kors will always be my first love. He gives great purse."

Rocco nods, picking up his glass of wine and tilting it in my direction. "Amen, sister."

Charlotte huffs. "Ava, stop being difficult and talk to us. I know it's a scary thing to be in love for the first time, but it's also amazing. Tyler is a nice guy. Sure, he's got a few kinky fetishes, but who cares? He's in love with you and he treats you better than any guy you've ever been with."

I will not drunk cry, I will not drunk cry.

"Who doesn't have kinky fetishes?" Rocco asks. "I once dated a guy who could only get it up if I played track ten on the *Oklahoma* soundtrack. Do you know what track ten is on the *Oklahoma* soundtrack? It's 'The Farmer and the Cowman.' As soon as he heard the words 'One man likes to push a plough, the other likes to chase a cow,' he would come like a wild man. He gave great head, so who was I to argue?"

My Little Pony suddenly doesn't seem so bad now.

"Who ordered this shit?!" I yell, staring down at my plate of pasta and refusing to talk about Tyler's fetishes.

"Be a good girl and eat your food," Charlotte tells me calmly.

I can't find my silverware and it suddenly occurs to me that I haven't eaten all day and I'm starving. I'm in love with hungry and I'm Tyler drunk.

Fuck it.

Rocco and Charlotte pause with their forks by their mouths to stare at me. I stare right back as I smack my hand down on the plate and scoop up and handful of rigatoni, splattering noodles and sauce all over the white tablecloth.

"I'm in love with drunk," I announce as I shovel noodles into my mouth.

"Is she seriously eating with her hands right now?" Rocco whispers in shock.

I ignore him, smacking my hand back down on the plate while I stare the two of them down. "I love hungry drunk!"

I notice a few patrons looking over at our table and I realize I'm probably being a little loud.

"This shit is delicious and I'm love drunk! Go fuck your face!" I shout at one woman in particular who is looking at me in disgust.

"Okay there, drunky, calm down," Charlotte says quietly, reaching over and placing her hand on my arm. "It's okay to admit it, you don't have to be afraid."

Rocco nods his head in agreement and all of a sudden, I feel like a weight has been lifted off my chest. Everything is going to be okay. I can be honest with my sister and my friend; they won't judge me.

I grab a few more noodles with my fingers and push them past my lips before taking a huge breath and letting it all out.

"I like to masturbate on the interstate!" I announce loudly.

Rocco's fork crashes to his plate and Charlotte starts choking on her glass of wine.

At this point, I can feel all eyes in the restaurant on me and I don't care. Fuck all of them!

"When I'm driving down the interstate, I just can't help it. All that open road and freedom makes me horny and I just have to do it. Every. Single. Time. Sometimes, I drive on the rumble strips at the edge of the road for miles because it makes me feel tingly."

I'm pretty sure I'm supposed to be talking about something else right now, but I don't remember what it is.

Fuck, this pasta is DELICIOUS.

"Oh, dear God," Charlotte whispers.

I smile at both of them and start licking sauce off of my fingers, lifting my feet up and resting them on Rocco's thigh.

"WHERE THE FUCK DID THESE SHOES COME FROM?" I yell, staring at my feet.

"I think it's time to get Interstate home to bed," Rocco announces, sliding my feet off of his lap as he stands.

Charlotte gets up from her chair, walks over to my side of the table and starts wiping my face with my napkin. "I know you're really drunk right now, but tomorrow when you're sober, you're going to be so happy that you finally realized you're in love with Tyler."

She helps me up from my seat and holds my arm as we walk out of the restaurant while Rocco pays the bill. I rest my head on her shoulder, letting her lead me out the front door. I can feel my throat getting tight and I squeeze my eyes closed to stop the tears from falling down my cheeks.

"Charlotte?"

"Yes, Interstate?" she replies with a laugh.

"I don't want these ugly fucking shoes on my feet!" I wail.

CHAPTER 20

Fisting - For the Win

- Tyler -

"You can't propose to Charlotte by just handing her a puppy, it's boring. Big mistake. Big. HUGE!" I yell, taking a sip of my beer.

"I'm really concerned that you just quoted *Pretty Woman*," Gavin states with a shake of his head.

"Dude, that's every guy's dream. Get a hooker for the night and then keep her forever without having to pay by the hour."

Gavin sets his bottle down and stares at me. "That is NO man's dream."

"You're out of touch with reality, my friend. It's every man's dream, they just don't like to talk about it," I explain. "I'm breaking the silence! HOOKERS ARE PEOPLE TOO!"

While Ava and Charlotte went out with Rocco tonight for some girl time, Gavin and I decided to stay in so he could drum up some proposal ideas. So far, all of them suck ass, so I called in reinforcement to help him out. I mean really, this is going to be one of the biggest days of his life. He needs help.

"Alright, I've got jumper cables, ten quarts of BBQ sauce and a really nice rhinestone tiara that we could take apart and shape into a ring," Drew announces as he walks through Gavin's front door, his arms full of bags.

He kicks the door closed behind him and dumps everything in the middle of the living room.

"I already bought Charlotte a ring, we don't need to make one," Gavin says, getting up from the couch to look through the bags.

"Fine, be a snobby little bitch. I'll have you know I make beautiful decoupage rings out of Polymer Clay, rubber cement and Mod Podge," he announces proudly.

Gavin ignores him, reaching into a bag and pulling out the largest flesh-colored rubber fist I've ever seen. He holds it up in the air staring at it while the thing flops back and forth.

"What the ever living fuck is this?" Gavin asks. "Please tell me this is not an actual FISTING fist."

Drew smiles and walks over to Gavin, grabbing the fist out of his hand. "This is Duke. He's a member of the family and he wants to help with the proposal."

Drew shakes the fist in front of Gavin's face. "Say hi to Duke."

Gavin scrunches up his face and moves away from the rubber fist. "I swear to God if that thing is one of yours and Aunt Jenny's sex toys I am going to puke all over this floor."

Drew pulls Duke close to his chest and looks at Gavin in shock. "I would NEVER defile Duke like that."

He holds the fist up to his face and speaks in a baby voice. "Don't you listen to big, bad Gavin, Duke. Daddy loves you."

"Where in the hell did you even get that thing?" I ask, staring in awe at Duke. If it wasn't so creepy looking, it really would be a thing of beauty. When I say it's a fist, I mean it's a fucking fist from elbow to fingers. That thing has got to be at least twelve inches long and six inches in diameter.

"Jenny and I rescued him from a sex toy mill," Drew tells us.

"I'm sorry, a what?" Gavin asks.

"A sex toy mill. It's like a puppy mill but worse. All of these sex toys crammed into boxes with no light or air, just waiting to die. It was so hard to just save one when there were so many who could use our help, but we saw Duke and we knew he had to come home with us," Drew explains, hugging Duke a little tighter to himself.

"Oh, sweet Jesus, that thing was a USED sex toy?" Gavin yells, scrambling up from the floor and moving as far away from Drew as possible.

Drew quickly sets Duke on the coffee table so he's standing straight up in the air and covers his hands over Duke's closed fist. "SHHHHHH! Not so loud, asshole! We don't like to talk about Duke's horrific past."

Drew goes over to the couch and flops down on the cushions. "So, I was thinking Duke could help you out with the proposal. He just had a manicure and he has an appointment for a facial tomorrow."

I laugh. "Let me guess, a cream pie facial?"

Gavin dry heaves and Drew shakes his head at me.

"He lived that long, lonely life for far too long, Tyler. Duke is on to bigger and better things."

Drew turns to Gavin who is currently pressed up against the far wall of the living room, as away from Duke as possible. "So, I was thinking. We could tie a ribbon around Duke's neck with the stupid ring you BOUGHT from a store and you could hold him out to Charlotte. We've been practicing his 'serene' face and I totally think he's got it down."

While Drew and Gavin start arguing about Duke being a part of the proposal, I pull my phone out of my pocket and try not to be disappointed that I don't have any drunk texts from Ava. Drunk texts are the best, especially when she totally forgets her aversion to anal and begs for it.

"Fisting is NOT romantic!" Gavin shouts from across the room, interrupting me from my thoughts.

"Duke is a very romantic person and it's going to hurt his feelings if he can't be part of this special day!" Drew yells back.

I pull up a video on my phone and walk over to Gavin. "See? Duke is a star. From the look on that chick's face, I'd say she's very happy to have Duke in her...life. And her vagina. Oh, look at that, and her ass!"

Gavin pushes my hand away. "That thing is not coming anywhere near Charlotte."

I stare at the video on my phone. "You're right, but I'm pretty sure *Charlotte* would be coming *everywhere* near that thing."

Drew laughs and rushes over to me for a high-five. "It's like we share a brain or something, dude."

Gavin groans. "You two are insane. I am getting a puppy and tying the ring on a ribbon around its neck, end of story."

Drew grabs Duke from the table and points it at Gavin. "You are a pussy. Duke is the most romantic person in the world. I can't believe you're saying no to him."

Gavin looks towards me for some help and I just shrug. "He's got a point. You are kind of a pussy and Duke is growing on me. I kind of want to take him out for drinks and sit him up in the middle of the table so he can wave at people that walk by."

"It might have to wait a few days," Drew informs me. "We were just at a club last night and Duke's still a little hung-over. He also wasn't happy that they had to stamp his hand on the way in. That ink was a bitch to scrub off this morning, wasn't it Duke?"

Gavin finally pushes away from the wall to cross his arms in front of him and glare at me. "If we're going to talk about pussies, how about we discuss the fact that you are in love with Ava but you're too chicken shit to tell her."

Drew stares at me with wide eyes, holding Duke up right in front of my face. "Oooooooh, burn!"

"I am NOT in love with Ava," I scoff.

Right? I'm not in love with Ava. Why would I be in love with someone who doesn't even like me?

"You've checked your phone fifteen times in the last half hour looking for a missed call or a text from her," Gavin accuses.

"Dude! I just don't want to miss out on drunk anal!" I argue.

Drew pulls Duke away from me and scratches the top of his head with Duke's fist. "Good call. Drunk anal is awesome."

"She told Charlotte you guys talked about your dad and that she opened up to you about how much she hates her job. Ava doesn't talk to people about shit like that unless she really trusts them and cares about them, and I'm pretty sure you wouldn't talk about your dad issues with just anyone," Gavin says.

"Awwww, do you have daddy issues?" Drew asks with a laugh.

I punch him in the arm. "Fuck you, I don't have daddy issues."

"He found out his dad isn't his real dad, and that his mom was a slut," Gavin tells Drew.

"Ahhhh, I love sluts," Drew muses.

"Why don't you just admit that you're in love with Ava?" Gavin questions, both of us ignoring Drew as he uses Duke to scratch his ass.

"Why don't you use Duke to propose to Charlotte?" I fire back.

"I'll make you a deal. I'll use Duke in my proposal if you tell Ava you love her."

The room is silent while Gavin and I stare each other down.

After a few seconds, I hold my hand out to him and he takes it. "Deal."

Drew places Duke on top of our joined hands and wraps his free arm around Gavin's shoulder.

Shit, what the fuck have I gotten myself into? I'm scared shitless to even think about the fact that I might be in love with Ava and now I have to come right out and tell her? I have to do it though. I have to get my feelings in check because it is absolutely imperative that Duke is a part of this proposal.

"This is the happiest day of Duke's life!" Drew announces as he squeezes Gavin's shoulder in excitement. "FISTING, FOR THE MOTHER FUCKING WIN!"

Duke – 1, Tyler - O

CHAPTER 21

All the Feels

~ Ava ~

"Dude, get a camera."

"Is this heaven? Did we die?"

"Seriously, get a fucking camera!"

Whispers from across the room bring me awake and I immediately regret opening my eyes when I'm hit with the bright morning light streaming in through the window.

I am never drinking again.

"Don't make any sudden movements or they'll scatter like wild animals," I hear Tyler whisper.

Ignoring the pounding in my head, I squint and look down at myself.

"Why am I naked?" I speak with a raspy, hung-over voice.

Feeling an arm tighten around my waist, I look over my

shoulder, watching Charlotte yawn before opening her eyes and staring right at me.

"Are you naked?" she asks in confusion, pulling back and looking between us. "Jesus Christ! Why am *I* naked too?"

Scooting away from her, I finally notice we're both curled up on the floor in between the couch and the coffee table. Empty bottles of beer and vodka are spread all around us, including one dead soldier of vanilla vodka shoved into the couch cushions. Memories of last night after we left the restaurant and came back here float through my mind. Charlotte, Rocco and I all got into a cab, stopped at a liquor store and then spent the rest of the night drinking ourselves into oblivion. Well, I was already there and by the state of undress between Charlotte and I, it looks like she followed very quickly. I have a vague recollection of Rocco telling us vaginas were gross and we felt the need to prove him wrong.

Where the fuck is Rocco?

"It's like porn and Christmas morning, all rolled into one," Tyler whispers in wonder.

Charlotte, finally realizing where we are and that we're not alone, screams so loud I have to cover my hands over my ears to stop my head from exploding.

"TYLER! Turn around! Turn around right now and stop staring at me!" she shouts, attempting to cover her boobs and crotch with her hands while she frantically yanks the couch cushions off and holds them in front of her.

"Jesus, could you guys keep it down? I've got the *worst* headache ever," Rocco complains, stepping out of the kitchen, holding his hand against his head.

"OH MY GOD WHY ARE YOU NAKED?!" Tyler screams, covering his eyes. "I JUST SAW A GAY PENIS! MAKE IT GO AWAY, MAKE IT GO AWAY!"

Oh, that's right. Rocco felt left out after Charlotte and I got naked.

Rocco laughs and leans against the doorframe. "Honey, my penis is the same as yours."

With his hands still shielding his eyes, Tyler shakes his head frantically back and forth. "FALSE! My penis prefers the pink and yours likes the stink. Put that thing away!"

Rocco sighs and goes in search of his pants.

Unlike my sister, I'm not one to shy away from nudity and I couldn't care less who's in this living room right now. I need water and aspirin STAT.

Pushing myself up from the floor, I work out the kinks in my neck resulting from a night spent on the floor and head towards the kitchen.

As I walk past Gavin and Tyler, Gavin averts his eyes from me and Tyler smacks him in the arm.

"I told you not to make any sudden movements. Now our chance of seeing real-life sister porn is ruined and filled with gay penis. RUINED!"

Gavin rushes over to Charlotte and helps her up from the floor and down the hall to their bedroom. While I rummage through their cupboards for a bottle of aspirin, Tyler comes up behind me and wraps his arms around my waist.

"So, I was thinking-"

"No, Charlotte and I will not recreate that scene for you later tonight," I interrupt him as I find the bottle, unscrew the top and shake three pills into my hand.

Tyler moves away from me, grabbing a glass from the counter and filling it up with cold tap water. He hands it to me and smiles. "Even though I believe you should seriously reconsider, I was actually going to suggest something else."

I pop the pills in my mouth, grab the glass from his hand and chug the entire thing. He takes the empty glass from my hands, refills it and hands it back. My heart stutters as he reaches out and slides his hand down the top of my head before cupping my cheek.

"Ava, will you go on a date with me?" he asks softly as he stares into my eyes.

Everything that happened last night with Charlotte and Rocco comes rushing back - the missing shoe, shoveling pasta in my mouth with my hands and the fact that I can't deny my feelings for Tyler any longer. Standing in the middle of my sister's kitchen without a stitch of clothing on, I suddenly feel more naked than I ever have in my entire life. I really do love this guy, as crazy as it sounds. I should tell him, I should just blurt it out like it's no big deal so we can move on and this moment won't be so uncomfortable anymore.

"A date? Are you serious?" I say instead.

Tyler nods, leaning in to place a kiss on my forehead. "Yep, a real date. I want to do something special with you, Ava. We can do whatever you want, as long as it's just the two of us."

I close my eyes as his lips leave my forehead and change my

mind about blurting how I feel about him right now when I'm naked and have the hangover from hell. I suddenly realize I want to do something special for him, as well, something to show him how I feel so that when I do finally get the courage to tell him, it will be *extra* special.

Leaning up on my tiptoes, I kiss his cheek. "I think that's a great idea. Don't make any plans for tonight around seven o'clock."

Putting the finishing touches on the table, I stand back to admire my work. Not too shabby for someone who just learned how to cook today, if I do say so myself.

"Alright, the lasagna has about five minutes left to cook. When the timer goes off, take it out and let it sit on the counter for about another fifteen minutes before you cut into it," Molly tells me as she comes out of our parent's kitchen.

Thank God for my baby sister. Being in culinary school, she was able to stop by in between classes and help me whip up dinner since I'm pretty much clueless in the kitchen unless I'm baking dessert. Molly is majoring as a pastry chef, but she's a genius with food no matter what she's making. She also let me know that our parents are out of town for two days so that I could sneak over here and have a quiet night alone with Tyler without having to worry about Gavin or Charlotte interrupting us.

I turn around to thank her for her help and she's already

disappeared like the ninja she is. With a shake of my head, I look down at myself to make sure I didn't get any food on my new dress. All of this – having a romantic date, cooking dinner for someone I love so I can tell him I love him – it's all new to me, so obviously that required a new dress. Luckily, Nordstrom's sent over a new Jessica Simpson black and white scallop lace tiered dress for me to blog about yesterday. Not cut nearly low enough and far from slutty, it isn't a dress I would normally wear, but it's perfect for tonight. It's simple and elegant and I feel pretty. It's nice to feel pretty once in a while, especially when you're gearing up to pour your heart out to a guy and hoping he doesn't laugh in your face.

The doorbell rings and I take a moment to give one last look at the beautifully set table, ensuring everything is in place. I rush to the door and open it to find Tyler standing there in black dress pants and a white button-down shirt. I've never seen him in anything but a t-shirt and jeans and this is a sight to behold. It takes me a full minute to recover the breath he's stolen so I can speak, but he beats me to it.

"You take my breath away, Ava Gillmore."

I giggle like a little girl and for once, I'm not even ashamed to admit it.

"You're looking mighty fine yourself, Tyler Branson," I tell him, holding the door open for him.

Closing the door behind him, I take a few slow breaths to try and calm my racing heart. I am so out of my element here. I should have asked Charlotte to stand outside in the shrubs next to an open window so she could feed me my lines all night.

When I turn around, he's clutching a square box in his hands that has a big red bow on it.

"I figured flowers were a bit too tame for a woman with sex toys in her blood and the rubber fisting mitten is just better suited for a second date, so this will have to do," he explains, holding the box out for me to take.

With a smile I can't contain, I grab the box and untie the bow. Lifting the lid, my eyes widen in surprise and my jaw drops when I see what's inside.

"I hope those are the right ones. I remember you saying you'd been trying to get them for months but they were sold out everywhere," he tells me quickly, taking the box back and pulling out the most beautiful pair of shoes I've ever seen.

"Christian Louboutin black suede Strass Decorapumps with Swarovski crystals," I mumble in awe as I reach out and lovingly pet the shoes Tyler holds in his hands. "How in the hell did you find these?"

I watch as he gets down on one knee and wraps his hand around my calf, lifting my foot up to his bent leg so he can remove the black patent leather Mary Janes I put on earlier. He slides the Louboutin on my foot and I suddenly feel like Cinderella. He does the same with my other foot and then stands back up to admire his work.

"Damn, your legs look fucking hot in those things," he says with a whistle.

"Seriously, Tyler, how did you find these and how did you afford them?" I demand.

I don't mean to sound ungrateful or anything, but these shoes were even out of *my* price range and I'm a shoe whore.

"You'd be surprised what the guys in the warehouse at work can get their hands on," Tyler explains as I walk around the foyer, testing out my new shoes. "Bill knows a guy who knows a guy. I'm pretty sure they're stolen and quite possibly have the previous owner's blood on them, but I didn't figure you'd mind. Felicia asked me if I wanted any meth and Rob told me he could get his hands on some whale sperm. I passed on the meth but I'm seriously considering the whale sperm."

I don't even bother to question the absurdity of the need for whale sperm, instead launching myself into Tyler's arms and peppering his face with kisses.

"This is just...I don't even know what to say. I love... these shoes. I love them so much it scares the hell out of me," I tell him, completely chickening out.

I have the feels. I have all the fucking feels and I can't say it!

He wraps his arms around me and smiles. "It's okay, babe. My love for these shoes freaks me out a little bit, too. They are *fantastic* and totally hot shoes. I've grown really attached to the...shoes."

Oh, my God. What is he saying? Is he feeling all the feels with me?

Before I can analyze his statement, he pulls back and grabs my hand. "It smells amazing in here, what's for dinner?"

I can do this. I can totally do this. I'll wow him with my delicious food and when he's in a food coma, I'll tell him that I love him.

Piece of cake.

CHAPTER 22

No Kink? No Problem.

- Tyler -

"I never meant to put him in an *actual* coma! Oh fuck, I killed him, didn't I?!"

Blinking my eyes open, I look up to see Ava pacing back and forth next to my hospital bed and I can't help but smile.

"He's going to be just fine. The important thing is that you got him here in time. As soon as we make sure he doesn't have any adverse reaction to the epinephrine we gave him, you can take him home and he'll be good as new."

I watch the doctor pat Ava on the back and give her a sympathetic look before leaving the room. She turns to look at me, her face lighting up when she sees that I'm awake.

"Tyler! Oh, thank fuck you're awake!" she exclaims, rushing to my side and placing her hands on either side of my face. "I'm so sorry. I swear I wasn't trying to kill you."

Laughing at her worry for me, I grab her arm and pull her closer until she's leaning over top of me. "Ava, it's fine. You had no way of knowing that I'm allergic to pine nuts."

She reaches up and runs her fingers through my hair and I have to fight really hard not to purr like a fucking cat.

"It's all Molly's fault. I had her help me make the lasagna and she had to be all fancy and shit with her sauce instead of just using something out of a jar," she says with a roll of her eyes.

I hate that Ava is so upset over this and I feel like shit for ruining the evening she planned. I knew as soon as I walked into the dining room and saw the table set with good china and lit candles that she put a lot of effort into making the dinner special and romantic. It's not her or Molly's fault that two bites of the delicious lasagna had me breaking out in hives and gasping for air as my throat closed up. Normally, I carry an EpiPen on me at all times because of this stupid allergy, but I was too worried about the gift I got her and trying to figure out a way to tell her that I love her to worry about a fucking nut allergy.

"Seriously, don't beat yourself up about it. It's not like I go around advertising the fact that eating pine nuts might kill me. Also, I'm really sorry about puking on your shoes in the parking lot," I tell her sheepishly.

She just shrugs and rests her head on my chest as she slides her body onto the small hospital bed next to me. "I don't care about the shoes, I'm just glad you're okay."

It's so quiet in the room you can hear a pin drop. Ava saying she cares more about me than a pair of fancy shoes is the equivalent of her telling me she loves me. I know it, and I'm pretty sure she knows it by the way she refuses to raise her head and look up at me. This is epic, like seriously mother fucking epic, and I really want to pull the curtain closed around us and strip her naked.

"So anyway," she finally says, ignoring the puke-stained shoes in the room. "The doctor said you'll be discharged within the hour, as soon as the I.V. bag of saline empties and you're feeling okay."

I clasp my hands together against her back and kiss the top of her head. I want to tell her I love her, but doing it in a hospital bed so soon after she had to see my body covered in red hives while I clutched at my throat gasping for breath doesn't seem appropriate.

"When we get out of here, we should take a shower," I tell her as she snuggles closer to me.

"Someone's obviously feeling better," she replies with a laugh. "If you're talking kinky, I think you'll be just fine."

Resting my head back on the pillow while I hold her close, I contemplate the perfect way to tell her I love her.

"Kinky is definitely good, but…you smell a little like puke. We should probably take care of that first."

"So, what's it going to be tonight? Do I need to get out the lube or lay a drop cloth down?" Ava asks with a laugh.

After I was discharged from the emergency room with a

reminder to avoid pine nuts in the future, we came back to Ava's parents' house and took a quick shower to wash away the smell of vomit. As hard as it was, I wouldn't let myself touch Ava in the shower no matter how much I wanted to. Shower sex is good and all, but not what I had in mind for tonight. Even though I ruined dinner by yacking all over her new shoes, I still want this night to end on a special note.

Resting my hands behind my head as I lay on her bed completely naked, I watch as Ava walks into the room with a towel wrapped around her. She rummages through the top drawer of her dresser and I lift up on my elbows to see what she's looking for.

"There's no point putting clothes on since I plan on ripping them right off in about five seconds," I laugh.

She steps into a pair of underwear and slides them up her thighs and under the towel. "Well, too bad. I bought new underwear for tonight so you're just going to have to suck it up."

I lick my lips as she reaches up and takes the clip out of her hair from the shower, her long hair tumbling down around her shoulders.

"Jesus, you are so fucking beautiful," I mutter as she runs her fingers through her hair.

She smiles at me, the tips of her fingers tracing over the cleavage peeking out of the top of the towel.

Anything else I might have said to her dies in my throat when she pulls the towel off and drops it to the floor.

I swallow thickly as she walks to the end of the bed in nothing but a black lace thong. She climbs up the end of the bed on her hands and knees, crawling over my body until she's straddling my thighs.

"You didn't answer my question," she says softly, leaning over me to rest her arms on either side of my head. "Ball gag, rubber body suit, Star Wars light saber dildo? What shall it be tonight?"

Her long hair falls around our faces like a curtain as I stare up at her. Removing my hands from behind my head, I grab onto her hips and roll us over without saying a word.

She gasps in surprise as I settle myself between her legs, shifting my hips so my cock slides right against the lacy material of her underwear.

"No toys tonight. Nothing weird, nothing kinky... just us," I tell her softly, holding myself above her.

Her brow furrows as she stares up at me. Reaching down, I slide one hand down the outer side of her thigh and pull it up over my hip. She places her hands on either side of my face, pulling me down to her lips. This kiss is unlike any kiss we've ever shared before and it suddenly occurs to me that maybe it's not that big of a deal if I don't have the words to tell her I love her. Actions speak louder and all that shit. Her tongue gently slides against my own and she tastes so fucking amazing that I groan and deepen the kiss.

Letting go of her thigh, I bring my hand between us, sliding my fingers through the edge of her thong at the juncture of her thighs and pulling it to the side. I thrust my hips slowly and slide my cock against her until I'm completely coated in her wetness and want to cry like a fucking baby at how good it feels.

Ava lifts her hips as she gently sucks my tongue into her mouth, forcing the tip of my cock to slide into her. I freeze, holding completely still and pulling my mouth away from hers.

"Condom, we need a condom," I gasp as she moves her hips again, pushing me a little deeper inside of her.

Her hands slide up into my hair and grasps onto chunks of it.

"In a minute. This feels really good. *You* feel really good," she whispers, pulling me back down to her mouth.

Making sure to keep myself still so I don't accidentally slam all of the way inside of her without protection, I kiss her again. Ava isn't having any of that, though, and she starts to move her hips frantically against me, trying to pull me in deeper, whimpering against my mouth.

"Fucking hell, Ava… your pussy feels so Goddamn good," I mutter, locking down every fucking muscle I have to hold still while she continues to lift her hips and the tip of my cock slides in and out of her.

"Say it again, fuck, say it again," she demands, raising her hips higher so my dick disappears a little further inside of her.

It's my turn to whimper as I feel more of her heat wrap around me. There's no fucking way I'm going to be able to move away from her body now. No fucking way.

"I love the way you feel. I don't want to stop," I tell her honestly.

She quickly moves her hands down to my ass and grabs on. I can't take the torture anymore and immediately relax.

"Then don't stop, it's okay, I'm on the pill and I trust you."

Her quietly whispered words and the way she's looking up at me is my complete undoing. I let out a shaky breath and slowly push my way inside of her.

We both groan when our hips meet and it takes me a minute to get used to the feel of being completely bare and completely inside of her. I've never felt anything this amazing in my life and I don't know how I'm going to last long enough to make this any good for her.

I bury my head in the side of her neck and breathe in the clean scent of her skin, pulling myself out of her and then sliding right back in. She runs her hands up my back and I shiver when I feel her nails lightly graze my skin. There's no way I can hold back at this point and I whisper words of apology to her as I start thrusting my hips. I should probably slow down long enough to remove the lace thong she put on for me, but I can't even be bothered with that. Now that I'm inside of her, I'm never leaving.

"Goddamn, baby," I whisper against her ear. This experience is so surreal that I just want to mumble and curse and call her every sweet name I can think of.

Ava wraps her arms around my back and locks her ankles together against my ass, using her heels to push me deeper inside of her as she lifts her hips to meet my thrusts.

I never thought vanilla sex would be something I'd like. I've always gotten off on crazy shit and scoffed at the simple stuff. I should have known sex with Ava, no matter what kind it is, would be anything but vanilla *or* simple. Listening to her chant my name as her orgasm approaches and dropping all of our barriers, the latex kind *and* the emotional kind, makes this the best fucking kind of sex in the entire world.

As I move faster and harder against her, she lifts her hands above her head, grabbing tightly to the wooden posts of the headboard. She tilts her head back and tightens her legs around me as she comes. Feeling her pulsing around my dick throws me right over the fucking edge. Smacking my hand down on the bed and clutching tightly to the sheet, I push myself as deep as I can go and lose myself inside of the woman I love.

This night could have turned to complete shit after everything that happened. As I collapse on top of Ava and we breathe heavily against one another, I smile, happy about the fact that some throw-up and a mild case of hives didn't ruin our first date.

If we can handle that, we can handle damn near anything.

CHAPTER 23

I Made a Poopy!

~ Ava ~

"This was the worst proposal idea in the history of the world," I complain, kicking my boot through a pile of snow as we trudge through the back yard.

"Whose idea was this anyway?" Tyler grumbles, walking next to me.

"Aren't you glad your parents went on that swingers cruise and you got to spend Christmas with us instead?" I ask with a laugh.

"Do NOT remind me of all the disgusting things my parents are most likely doing out at sea," he complains.

"Gives new meaning to the words 'wet discharge' doesn't it?" Uncle Drew shouts.

We both stop and stare over at the edge of the lawn where a clump of bushes hides him.

"That's the name of my future boat, by the way," he adds.

Tyler and I both shake our heads in disgust and continue pacing around the yard.

After much consideration with the family, Gavin decided the perfect idea for proposing to Charlotte would be to buy her a puppy and tie the ring on a red ribbon around the puppy's neck. Super sweet idea until you realize that puppies are stupid and will eat anything. The trial run Gavin did resulted in the puppy eating the entire red ribbon and the fake, plastic ring he attached to it for practice.

Gavin promptly took the puppy back to the pet store and got a refund, failing to mention to the owner that there could be a shit surprise for him the next morning.

He decided to go with plan B, which sounded like a much better idea at the time. Unfortunately, no one passed that memo along to Uncle Drew.

"How long does it take you to shit, old man?" Tyler yells in the direction of the bushes.

I stare at him, trying to give myself an extra boost of courage to tell him that I love him.

It's not that hard, Ava, just fucking say it!

After what happened between us the other night after the trip to the emergency room, this should be the easiest thing in the world. I really thought life would Tyler would be all about the crazy, weird shit we'd do in the bedroom. He can definitely fuck like a boss when he gets kinky, but I feared it would get a little old, especially if I had to Google half the stuff he wanted to do. Knowing he can also make the sweetest love in the history of the world, as well as pull off the best dirty talk I've ever heard, solidified my feelings for him. If I didn't think it was completely cliché to tell him I love him during our post-coital glow, I would have done it then. I *should* have done it then. Having a few days to think about it and plan it out has just fucked with my nerves.

"A proper shit takes time, my friend. You just slow your roll and go grab me a magazine or something," Uncle Drew yells back, the branches of the shrubs rustle as he does God knows what back there.

Aunt Claire came up with the idea that Gavin should bake Charlotte cupcakes and hide the ring in one of them. Again, super sweet idea, until Uncle Drew saw them sitting on the counter and ate every single one. Whole. Just shoveled each one in his mouth until Gavin walked into the kitchen and started screaming. Tyler and I had to calm him down and get both him and Uncle Drew out of the house before Charlotte figured out what was going on.

"Just so you know, when he *does* go to the bathroom, I am NOT digging through his pile of shit for a diamond ring. There's a lot of things I'll do for diamonds, but that is not one of them."

Dammit! What is wrong with me? Just say it. Say, "I love you, Tyler."

"This problem could be solved in a minute if Duke were here," Tyler mumbles to himself.

"Duke? Who's Duke?" I question.

"Don't worry, Duke is right here helping things along," Uncle Drew shouts from the bushes.

Tyler takes a deep breath, sticks his hands in his pockets, pulls them back out and then starts pacing nervously.

"Shit. Shit fuck damn! Ava, I need to tell you something," he starts, turning to face me.

I watch him bite his bottom lip and a wave of desire washes through me so quickly I have to catch my breath. I really do love him. He's sweet and cute and he's good to me.

"I need to tell you something too," I tell him excitedly, moving closer to his body.

Tyler reaches for me and we both open our mouths to speak at the same time when Uncle Drew starts cheering and shouting across the yard.

"IT'S HAPPENING! IT'S REALLY HAPPENING! I'M SHITTING IN THE SHRUBS!"

We move away from each other and do everything we can to avoid looking in Uncle Drew's direction.

"Uuuggghh, I don't have time for this. I need to get on a computer and order my BronyCon tickets before they're gone," Tyler grumbles.

"You're serious about doing this? You can't possibly think some random guy that could be your father would even go to this thing. How would you even know who he was when you got there?"

Tyler laughs and shakes his head at me. "Obviously if he's my dad, he'll be at this thing. I didn't just *turn* Brony, I was born this way."

"You're being absurd, Tyler. This isn't going to work," I tell him.

"This isn't about me finding my dad. This is about you not understanding me being a Brony. I knew you wouldn't be able to handle it."

Is he serious with this shit?

"Don't tell me what I can and can't handle. I think you're insane for believing you'll be able to go to some huge gathering of weird people and be able to immediately recognize your father," I argue.

Tyler crosses his arms in front of him and glares at me. "*Weird people?* Did you just call me weird? Oh, no you didn't!"

I hate that we're fighting outside in the freezing cold weather on Christmas, but his words hit too close to home and that pisses me off even more. I *don't* understand the whole Brony thing and I can't do anything but lash out.

"If the horse tail fits!" I fire back.

"You know what? At least I'm taking a risk. I'm going out on a limb and doing everything I can to find out who my father is so I can move on with my life. What about you, Ava? Are you just going to keep working at Seduction and Snacks for the rest of your life, making you and everyone else miserable in the process?"

I shake my head and turn away from him. "You don't understand."

Tyler grabs my arm and turns me around to face him. "You're right, I don't understand. You have enough sponsorship on your blog right this minute to quit the job you hate and do what you love.

You can make a living off of this and yet you're still going in to your mom's office every day, hating every minute of it. You need to tell your mom what's going on."

I shrug out of his hold and take a step back. "My mom doesn't understand, I told you that."

"So MAKE her understand, dammit! Let her know how much this means to you."

I put more distance between us, walking backwards through the snow.

"Stay out of it, Tyler. This is *my* life."

He's quiet for a few minutes and I watch him stand there in the middle of the yard. He slides his hands in his pockets and puffs of cold air float out of his mouth.

"You're afraid. You're afraid to quit Seduction and Snacks because it's safe. It's easy to stay there, doing what you're told every day instead of taking a chance on something new," Tyler says quietly.

I'm pretty sure he's not talking about work anymore.

"I am NOT afraid! I take plenty of chances. I took a chance on you, didn't I? I completely changed myself for some GUY and look where it got me? I'm standing outside in the snow on Christmas waiting for my uncle to take a shit," I yell angrily.

"I never asked you to change anything for me. I like you just the way you are; I just want you to be happy. I'm so sorry being with *some guy* couldn't make you a little less of a bitch."

Before I can fire off another insult that will most likely make me feel even worse than I already do, the back door opens and

Gavin comes rushing outside.

"Did he shit yet? I need that ring!"

Tyler glares at Gavin and I look away from both of them. Everything we said to each other is playing on a loop in my head and making me feel like the biggest asshole in the world.

"GAVIN! I MADE A POOPY!" Uncle Drew shouts as he comes running out from behind the bushes, buttoning his pants.

"Did you really just say that?" Tyler asks him with a shake of his head.

"Fuck your face! Now, who wants to dig through the epic dump I just took and get the ring?" Uncle Drew asks.

Tyler walks up to Gavin and pats him on the back. "You should have went with my idea of riding in on an Alpaca. Alpacas won't eat diamond rings."

I quietly walk away from the three of them and make my way to the back door. I want to tell Tyler that I didn't mean what I said, but I don't even know if it's true. I *don't* understand the whole Brony thing and I really *do* think he's nuts for thinking he can go to this thing and find his real dad. It's probably better if I just walk away right now. I don't like thinking about the fact that he's right and I am afraid. I'm not the type of person who has ever been afraid of anything in my life. I go balls to the wall with everything I do and I never let anyone make me feel bad about the choices I make. Not having my mom's approval to do something different with my life has affected me more than I care to admit. I hate that Tyler might be right and that I'll continue doing what's safe because I'm too scared to put my foot down with my mom.

"Somebody get me a pair of tongs and some rubber gloves," Gavin demands as I open the door to the house.

"I'd tell you this is the weirdest thing that I've seen in a long time, but I've seen skat porn. Watching you dig through shit is nothing compared to that," Tyler states as I walk into the house and try not to think about the fact that I might have just screwed up the best thing that's ever happened to me.

CHAPTER 24

Merry Kiss My Ass

- Tyler -

"WHAT THE FUCK DID YOU DO TO MY COOKIES?!"

Gavin and I pause by the kitchen sink, staring at each other in confusion as Claire's angry voice carries from the living room.

"Dude, what's wrong with your mom?"

Gavin shrugs, returning to the task of removing all traces of human feces from Charlotte's engagement ring.

"Who the hell knows? Just keep an eye out for Charlotte. She can't see this ring until it's time."

"You're seriously still going to give that thing to her? Dude, you should just chuck it and call it a loss. You can't put a ring on her finger that at one point in time was in your uncle's colon."

Gavin ignores me and continues to furiously scrub the ring wearing a pair of rubber gloves, soap and water flying everywhere. I continue with my guard duty, standing between Gavin and the door so I can block what he's doing from anyone who enters. I'm not going to think about the fact that Ava and I just had our first fight and now she won't even look at me, or the fact that the gift I bought her for Christmas is now a total bust. She'll probably burn it and laugh at my lame attempt to try and get her to understand me a little better.

Gavin's hand is suddenly in my face, the two carat diamond sparkling right by my nose. "Smell this. Does it smell like shit?"

"Eeeew! Get that thing away from me!" I shout, smacking his hand away as I turn to face him.

"Stop being a pussy and smell it!" Gavin argues.

"I don't want to smell it, YOU smell it!" I fire back.

"SMELL IT RIGHT NOW OR I WILL PUNCH YOU IN THE SACK!"

I hear a groan behind me and whip around to find Charlotte standing in the doorway with a disgusted look on her face. "Are you two smelling your fingers again?"

Throwing my arms out wide to cover Gavin, giving him time to pocket the ring, I smile at Charlotte. "Oh, my God, you caught us! We like smelling our fingers. What else would we smell? Smelling our fingers is fun. Do you want to smell my fingers?"

Gavin's elbow jabs into my spine and I quickly correct my last statement. "NO! Don't come over here. I'll come to you so you can smell my fingers."

Gavin curses quietly and Charlotte shakes her head. "You two are so weird. Gavin, you need to get in here. Your mom is having a breakdown about her Christmas cookies."

He sticks his head out next to mine. "Okay, honey! We'll be there as soon as we're finished in here!"

She gives us one last weird look before leaving the kitchen.

We both sigh in relief and I turn back around to look at Gavin

"Smelling our fingers is fun?" he asks with a roll of his eyes.

"Hey, it got her out of here, didn't it?"

"I'M GOING TO KILL ALL OF YOU ASSHOLES!"

Another scream from Claire has us hustling out of the kitchen and into the living room. The sight before us is a little crazy, but nothing we haven't seen before in this family. Claire is holding a tray of frosted Christmas cookies in one hand and using the other to throw them at Drew, Carter and Jim, all of whom are huddled on the floor in front of the tree covering their faces and laughing hysterically.

I look over at Ava questioningly, but as soon as our eyes meet, she quickly looks away. I should never have said those things to her. I crossed the line and now she's never going to speak to me again.

"Honey, calm down, it's not that big of a deal," Carter laughs as a cookie bounces off of his nose.

"YOU RUINED CHRISTMAS!" Claire screams.

"Hey, can I get everyone's attention? I have something important to say," Gavin says loudly, trying to calm the situation.

Liz gets up from the couch, walks over to Claire and pats her on the back. "The cookies aren't that bad."

Claire turns and thrusts the tray into Liz's face. "Not that bad?! There are bloody frogs in Santa's bag."

I can't help it. A loud laugh bursts out of me, but I quickly cover my mouth when Claire looks at me with rage in her eyes.

Gavin tries again, walking into the middle of the room. "Seriously, can everyone stop talking?"

"Hey, it was your idea to let the three of us finish decorating those cookies. What did you expect?" Drew asks.

"What did I expect? WHAT DID I EXPECT? I certainly *didn't* expect you assholes to shit on tradition by writing 'Merry Kiss My Ass' on my Christmas cookies!" Claire screeches like a banshee as she lobs a handful of cookies across the room.

Gavin drops to the floor to avoid getting smacked in the face and Drew squeals like a girl when a cookie hits him square in the chest. "Heeeey, don't break this one! It's my favorite. Do you know how long I spent making flesh-colored frosting to turn these stockings in to penises?"

Claire lets out a feral scream and prepares to launch herself over the table to attack Drew but is thwarted by Liz, who grabs her firmly around the waist to prevent bloodshed.

"In our defense, Drew brought over some of his special cookies and we may or may not have eaten two dozen of them between us before we started decorating," Jim explains.

"You three idiots ate pot cookies before you decorated Claire's Christmas cookies? What is wrong with you?" Liz asks in amazement.

"See? Now you know why I want to kill them," Claire adds.

Liz lets go of her hold on Claire and crosses her arms in front of her. "Exactly. They had pot cookies and didn't share with us."

Claire smacks her in the arm and Liz backpedals. "I mean, you three should be ashamed of yourself for ruining those cookies."

From his spot on the carpet, Gavin reaches out and picks up one of the fallen cookies. "Does this present cookie say 'To Gavin, from Chuck Norris?"

Claire and Carter make eye contact over Gavin's head and they both start laughing.

"Wait a minute. I remember when I was like ten, I got a bunch of presents for Christmas from weird people. Big Bird, Captain Spock, RuPaul and Satan," Gavin mutters.

This makes Claire and Carter laugh even harder.

"We may or may not have smoked a little pot that year under the Christmas tree while we wrapped your presents," Claire says in between giggles.

"Seriously, you guys? When I asked about it on Christmas morning you told me the elves were pissed at Santa because he didn't offer 401k," Gavin complains. "That's the year I stopped believing in Santa because you said he didn't have fair labor laws."

"We were probably high on Christmas morning, too," Carter says with a shrug.

Charlotte walks up to Gavin and offers her hand, helping him up from the floor.

"By the way, Claire, if you're looking for your rabbit vibrator, it's in the silverware drawer," Drew tells her casually as he gets up from the floor and drops himself onto the couch.

"What the hell are you talking about?" Claire asks. "Why were you anywhere near my rabbit?"

Drew shrugs and picks up a broken cookie resting on the cushion next to him. "Frosting cookies with a butter knife wasn't working for me so I went digging through the drawers in your bedroom. On the lowest setting with the beads swirling, the rabbit does a magical job of frosting cookies."

"I ate four of those cookies already!" Liz shouts, grabbing a napkin from the coffee table and wiping her tongue with it.

Gavin looks over at me and I'm fairly sure he's about ready to throw up. This is definitely not how he envisioned proposing to Charlotte, but he should have known better with his family.

"Dude, just do it. It can't possibly get any worse," I tell him.

Charlotte looks back and forth between us as Claire rushes over to the couch to strangle Drew. "Do it? Do what?"

Gavin takes a deep breath and gets down on his knee. The entire room goes silent and Charlotte's eyes go wide as Gavin digs into the front pocket of his pants.

He pulls out the ring and holds it up in front of him. "Charlotte, you are my best friend and I love you more than I ever thought possible. I want to spend the rest of my life kissing you goodnight and waking up to you every morning. Will you marry me?"

Charlotte doesn't miss a beat. She immediately starts jumping up and down screaming. "YES, YES, OH, MY GOD YES!"

She throws herself into Gavin's arms and everyone starts cheering and clapping as Gavin gets up from the floor.

"Well, what are you waiting for? Put the ring on her finger already!" Claire says excitedly.

Gavin looks down at the ring, up at Charlotte and then back down. "Um, I think I'll wait."

Charlotte holds her left hand out for him. "Don't be silly, put it on!"

Gavin pulls the ring in close to his chest. "No, really, I think you're going to want to wait to put this on."

She rolls her eyes at him, holding her palm out. "Give me the ring."

"No," Gavin shakes his head.

"Gavin, I want my ring."

He holds the ring tighter to his chest and continues shaking his head.

Oh, for the love of God.

"Charlotte, Drew shit out that ring about twenty minutes ago. It needs a good bleaching before it comes in contact with your finger," I tell her.

Gavin gives me a dirty look for spilling his secret and Charlotte's hand recoils in revulsion.

"Drew, I thought we decided a few years ago that putting jewelry up there was dangerous," Jenny scolds. "My mother still isn't happy that I haven't been able to return that strand of pearls I borrowed."

Everyone starts talking all at once while Gavin explains about Drew eating the cupcake with the ring inside. Ava has been quiet through this entire debacle and I can't help but stare at her across the room. She looks sad and I want to go to her, but I don't want to cause a scene in front of everyone right now. This is a happy moment for my best friend and I'm not going to ruin it by getting into another argument with Ava. I'm sure she just needs to cool off a little and then everything will be fine between us and we can go back to having amazing sex.

CHAPTER 25
Whinny Like a Horse
~ Ava ~

"Jenny, why do you have photos taped all over your wall?" Aunt Liz asks.

She wanders over to the wall in Aunt Jenny's office at Seduction and Snacks that is covered in pictures she took at Christmas.

"That's my Facebook wall where I post my pictures. See? I tagged you in the pictures you're in," she explains, pointing to a picture with a sticky note attached to it that says *Liz*. "Here, I'm sharing the pictures, too."

Aunt Jenny grabs a stack of pictures from her desk and starts passing them out to us.

"Jenny, honey, you know that's not how Facebook works, right?" Aunt Claire asks, looking up from the paperwork on her desk as Aunt Jenny drops a few photos in front of her.

Fed up with the moping I've been doing for the last few days, my mom asked me to come in to the original Seduction and Snacks store and help with paperwork instead of going in to the main headquarters. I wanted to protest, but coming here would be better than going in to the office where I might run into Tyler.

"I don't understand most of Facebook, but this I totally get. I just need to get some addresses so I can mail the pictures I want to share with other people. I'm going to mail them a friend request, too," Aunt Jenny smiles excitedly.

Pulling my cell phone out of my purse, I check my messages and can't help but feel like shit when I don't see any from Tyler. I thought for sure he'd text me apologizing or asking if we could try anal again... *something.* I haven't heard from him in three days. Three long days without arguing with him, listening to him say stupid things, feeling his hands on me, kissing him, being annoyed with him... why hasn't he contacted me?

"Ava, either call the boy and make up or find someone else and move on. Quit pouting and help us file these invoices," my mom scolds.

I give her a dirty look as I shove my phone back in my purse. "I wasn't pouting, especially over Tyler. I don't know what you're talking about."

She laughs and shakes her head at me. "I'm not as stupid as your Aunt Claire looks."

Aunt Claire gives her the finger. "Shut up or I'll cut off your dick and make you eat it."

"Anyway," mom continues, "even though the guy irritates me the majority of the time and the sounds I've heard coming from your bedroom make my ears bleed, I don't like seeing you so sad over him."

If only she knew that he isn't the only reason I'm sad. With a deep breath, I decide to listen to what Tyler said and try talking to her again. She's got to understand how miserable I am at Seduction and Snacks.

"Drew likes to make horse noises during sex sometimes. I thought it was weird at first but it's kind of hot now," Aunt Jenny muses. "Look, I even shared it on my wall."

She points to a hand-written piece of paper taped to the wall that says '*My husband likes to whinny like a horse during sex*'.

"Can you guys tell me you like it? No one ever likes what I post," she complains.

We all ignore her and I walk up next to my mom as she unpacks and stocks a delivery of lube. "So, I've been thinking about giving my notice at Seduction and Snacks."

"Hey, Claire, did you ever get a reply back from Channel 5 news about the feature they wanted to do on us?" she yells over to my aunt, completely ignoring me.

"They're going to come out next Thursday to film some footage. The interview will be on Friday," Aunt Claire answers.

I try again, a little louder this time. "I don't want to work at Seduction and Snacks anymore."

"Fuck, Jenny! Will you stop poking me in the side?" Aunt Claire complains from the other side of the room.

Aunt Jenny huffs and crosses her arms in front of her. "Why the hell do they have poking on Facebook if no one likes it? I poked a customer the other day and she smacked my hand."

Taking a cue from Aunt Jenny, I shove my finger into my mom's side until she yelps. "What the fuck, Ava? Don't tell me I need to explain Facebook to you, too. Jenny, for God's sake, you've given my child the dumb. Stop fucking poking people."

My mom and Aunt Claire share a laugh and I reach the end of my rope.

"I HATE WORKING AT YOUR FUCKING COMPANY AND I QUIT!"

The room goes silent after my outburst and I take a step away from my mom when she glares at me.

"That *fucking company* has kept a roof over your head and put you in designer clothes since birth," she says in a low, menacing voice.

It's never good when my mom lowers her voice. Never.

"Mom, I didn't mean-"

She cuts me off. "Without that *fucking company*, you wouldn't know the difference between a Coach purse and a pile of shit."

I continue backing away from her until I bump up against my Aunt Claire. She wraps her arms around me in a comforting hug and leans down to whisper in my ear. "I'll distract her with a dildo to the face. When she's down, RUN!"

My mom continues walking until we're toe-to-toe and I swallow nervously. "Your Aunt Claire and I worked our fucking fingers to the bone to make this company what it is today. People would KILL for the job you have and you want to just throw it away because you're *bored*? You should be ashamed of yourself."

I choke back tears as my mom stares at me in disappointment. I *should* be ashamed. This *is* a job opportunity that anyone would be thankful for and I *am* throwing it all away. I just want her to understand that I'm not throwing my job away because I'm ungrateful or because I'm bored. I'm doing it because I have different dreams. Why the hell is it so hard to say that to her?

"Hey, ease up, Liz. Not everyone is cut out to work at Seduction and Snacks," Aunt Claire says softly from behind me, giving me a reassuring squeeze on the arm.

"Not everyone *should* be cut out to work there, but my kids damn well should be! This is my dream, this is what I've worked my entire life for and is it so wrong I want my family to benefit from the good fortune we've had?" my mom asks her.

Her dream, her dream, her dream... I wish she would listen to herself.

"It's not wrong, hon. I'm not going to lie about the fact that I love having Gavin here. I love it even more that working here has always been his dream. That's just it, though. It's what *he's* always wanted to do," Aunt Claire tells her.

My mom rolls her eyes and turns away from both of us, stalking to the other side of the room to angrily dig into a box of furry handcuffs. "Ava has no idea what she wants to do aside from shop. If she wants to quit, fine, but she better not ever come crying to me about how she made a mistake."

She won't even look at me now and she's talking about me like I'm not standing right here. This went just as well as I imagined.

So much for taking Tyler's advice.

I shrug out of Aunt Claire's hold, grab my purse from the desk and leave before anyone can see me cry.

"Hey, Ava, I just posted on my wall that you quit. I already got one 'like'!" Aunt Jenny shouts as I walk out the door.

"It doesn't count if you just *say* you liked it," Aunt Claire tells her with a sigh.

Screw everyone. I don't need my mother's approval and I certainly don't need Tyler. I'll be just fine on my own.

CHAPTER 26

When You Wish Upon a Dildo

- Tyler -

I pace back and forth nervously outside of Liz's office, waiting for her to finish her conference call. I don't know what the fuck I'm doing, but I'm pretty sure I'm going to regret it.

Ava went back home to her parent's house Christmas night and we haven't spoken since. As much as I want to be pissed at her for the things she said, I can't. The more I thought about it, the more I realized she was probably right. I *was* delusional for thinking my dad could be some famous Brony and that I would be able to pick him out in a room filled with thousands of people. I wanted it to be true so badly that I didn't even stop to think about how far-fetched it sounds. I'm also in love with her and love makes you do asinine things.

After our fight in her parents' backyard, we stayed on opposite sides of the room for the rest of the night. We spent the remainder of the evening celebrating the holiday and toasting Gavin and Charlotte on their engagement before I walked out of there without even a wave good-bye from her.

That was a week ago. I was determined to walk away from her and chalk it up to us just not being meant for each other, but I know it's not true. Regardless of what I said to her, she's the strongest person I know. She's sweet and funny when she wants to be and I like being around her. No, fuck that. I love being around her. She gets my crazy fetishes even if she doesn't want to and she puts up with my childish behavior. I'm not about to let her wallow in her own misery.

"Come on in, Tyler," Liz shouts from inside the office.

I take a deep breath and walk through the doors, sitting down in one of the chairs on the other side of Liz's desk.

"If you came in here to demand I tell you where our masturbation room is, I'm going to stop you right there," she begins.

"Liz, one of these days you're going to be honest with me. I know this room exists and, as an employee of Seduction and Snacks, I think it's only right that you lead me to heaven."

She puts her elbows on her desk and her head in her hands.

"Actually, I'm here on a more important matter," I tell her.

She looks up and her eyes widen. "Wait, you actually want to talk about something other than the masturbation room that may or may not exist?"

I can't believe I'm doing this. Ava better appreciate this shit because I'm pretty sure I can get Liz to crack.

"I want to talk to you about Ava."

Liz sighs and leans back in her chair. "Well, good luck with that. I'm not too happy with Ava right now, so you're on your own with that one."

Gavin told me that Ava tried to talk to her mom the other day about quitting her job here and it turned into one big clusterfuck. I feel bad that I sort of pushed Ava into doing that and I want to make it right.

"Have you even looked at her blog lately?" I question her.

She picks up a pen and starts tapping it against her desk. "That jenky-looking thing she created on Wordpress with a couple of pictures of her in different outfits? Yes, I've seen it," Liz states sarcastically.

"It's not jenky anymore. She had Jenny create her a whole new site with graphics and it's pretty awesome. Did you know she gets more hits on that thing every day than the Seduction and Snacks website? I checked."

Liz stops tapping her pen and stares at me.

"She also has a shit ton of sponsors paying her for ads now. She's making more money on that blog than she makes here. This is what she's always wanted to do. Can you understand that?" I ask.

I hold my breath, waiting for her to vault over her desk and choke me out. Liz scares me just a little bit, but I need to keep going and say everything I came in here to say.

"Ava is smart and amazing and this blog she's doing, it's not just a hobby. It's something she really cares about and loves. She's been working her ass off on this blog. It's *real* for her. This is what she wants to do with the rest of her life. She loves shoes and clothes and all that other girly shit. Seduction and Snacks isn't her dream, it's yours. Her dream is to talk about all that girly shit and she's turned it into a good paying reality. She needs you to understand and to give her your approval. I'm sure not everyone was on-board with the whole sex-toy shop slash bakery when you and Claire dreamed it up. How would you feel if the most important person in your life belittled your dream?"

I stop and try not to wince as I brace for the explosion from Liz that I'm sure is imminent. Maybe I overstepped my bounds. Ava is *her* daughter and who the hell am I to tell her what to do?

Liz is quiet and still for so long that I'm a little worried I might have given her a heart attack. When she finally moves, it's to brush a tear off of her cheek.

Awwwww shit, I made her cry. This can NOT end well for me.

"She hates working here. I always thought it was because she was just being stubborn," Liz says quietly.

"Well, she is a stubborn ass, but that's not it."

Liz glares at me.

"I mean, she's an amazing, beautiful, wonderful, stubborn girl."

She leans forward and rests her elbows on her desk. "You're in love with her."

"WHAT? How do you know that? I just figured that out myself," I tell her in shock.

"Tyler, you came in here and pretty much told me I'm an idiot even though you knew there was a possibility I would beat the shit out of you for doing it," she explains. "If that isn't love, I don't know what is."

I smile at her. "See? I knew you'd totally understand how much of an idiot you've been."

"I can still cut off your dick and make you eat it," she states.

"Duly noted," I nod. "It doesn't matter, though, since I'm pretty sure she hates me."

Liz shakes her head in disagreement. "Ava has spent every day since Christmas crying in her room. I don't know what happened between you guys, but I'm pretty sure she's in love with you, too."

Ava's been crying? Ava knows how to cry? I don't even know how to process this information.

"I'm sure that has nothing to do with me. That's all your fault for shitting on her dream," I tell her.

"Don't ruin the good thing we have going on here, Tyler. I have a letter opener within reach that I'm not afraid to use on your balls," she threatens. "Even before we had our little fight the other day, she was a mess. I think she realized she's in love with you and screwed up."

Oh, God, please let her really be in love with me and I'll never jerk off to another episode of MLP ever again. Maybe. Probably. Shit. I'll try really hard.

"That fight was my fault. We got into it on Christmas and I sort of told her she was too scared to come out and tell you she doesn't want to work here anymore."

Liz lets out a low whistle. "Damn, and she didn't punch you in the throat for that? She's *definitely* in love with you if she let you get away with saying that to her."

She stares down at her hands for a few minutes before looking up at me. "She really doesn't want to work here?" Liz finally says with a sniffle.

I shrug. "No, she hates it here."

Her lip quivers and part of me wants to get up, walk around the desk and hug her, but there was this whole thing with Gavin's mom not that long ago where I sort of had the hots for her and that *really* didn't end well and I can no longer even *think* about the word 'cougar' without throwing up in my mouth just a little bit. I don't want Liz to get the wrong idea or anything.

I watch as Liz slides her laptop closer to her and starts clicking away on her keyboard. After a few seconds, her eyes widen and her mouth drops open.

"Oh, my God. This is her site? This thing is amazing," she says in awe.

I quickly get up and lean across the desk. "Yep, see all those ads on the right side of the page? Those companies are all paying her money to advertise on her site. And they send her free shit all the time to try on and tell people about."

Liz clicks through all of the pages and photos, making comments here and there. She stops when she gets to one picture and cocks her head to the side.

"Are you wearing a sparkly t-shirt, skinny jeans and black stilettos in this picture?" she asks.

"Hey, those pants were very slimming and if you'll look at all the comments, I was told those shoes made my calves look amazing," I tell her.

She clicks out of the picture and closes her laptop.

"I should probably cut off your balls for talking to me the way you did. I *do* have a reputation to uphold."

I slowly back away from the desk and cover my junk with my hands.

Liz gets up from her chair and rounds the desk as I continue to back up. She moves faster and grabs onto my arm, dragging me towards the door.

"Oh, God, what are you going to do to me? You know what? I probably deserve it, just try not to leave any scars on my face. I'd like to continue with my modeling career on the side if Ava ever forgives me. She just got in this great hat that I really think would look stellar on me."

We walk through the door and she continues to pull me down the hall and around a corner. She doesn't say a word to me until we get to the opposite end of the building and we're standing outside of a locked room. Liz pulls a set of keys out of her back pocket and unlocks the door.

"You are to tell NO ONE of this. This room doesn't exist and this never happened," she states as she pushes me into the room in front of her. "Tyler, welcome to the masturbation room."

It takes everything in me not to sink to my knees on the floor and start weeping.

"It's real. I knew it. I knew if I wished hard enough and

thought about it long enough, it would come true," I whisper as I stare through the two-way mirror.

I'm so overcome with joy that all I can do is sing. "When you wish upon a dildo…"

"Oh, Jesus God," Liz mutters as she backs out of the room while I continue to hum.

Dreams really do come true.

CHAPTER 27
Friendship is Magic
~ Ava ~

"Alright, time to stop being a vagina. Get your ass out of bed and take a fucking shower," Charlotte scolds as she barges in my room.

I stare at her in irritation as she goes digging through my dresser, tossing clothes at me.

"Oh, my God. I can't wear that shirt with these pants!" I complain.

Charlotte turns around to face me with a smile on her face. "There we go, that's the Ava I know and love."

I roll my eyes at her and flop back down on my pillows. I've done nothing but mope around the house since Christmas and then it just got worse after the fight with my mom. It's pathetic. I miss Tyler so fucking much and I want so badly to call him, but I'm sure he hates me. I haven't heard from him since we fought in the yard.

I'm a bitch and I'm never going to change.

"I have some news for you. You're going to want to sit up for this," Charlotte informs me, jumping onto the foot of my bed and curling her legs up under her.

"If it has anything to do with the fact that I've called off of work the last three days, don't bother. I've already gotten an earful from mom about my responsibilities as an adult," I tell her.

"Jesus, stop feeling sorry for yourself, asshole! You know you brought this on yourself, right? All you had to do was sit mom down and be honest with her. You're good at telling people off and sticking up for others, why is it so hard to do it for yourself?"

I roll over and face the wall, not wanting to look at her while she tells me how much I suck. I already got that memo.

"Well, lucky for you, there's no need to worry about mom. Tyler took care of it for you."

I bolt up in bed and kick the covers off. "What? What are you talking about?"

Charlotte smiles and leans back against the wall casually. "Tyler marched into mom's office this morning and basically told her off. He told her how smart and amazing you are and how your blog is your dream and she should be more understanding of what makes you happy. He actually made mom cry."

My mouth drops open in shock.

"Why would he do that?" I whisper.

"Because he gets a sick thrill out of seeing her weep like a baby."

I shake my head in irritation. "Not the crying, dick face. Why would he talk to her for me?"

Charlotte sits forward and tilts her head. "Um, probably because he's in love with you, moron. He knew you needed a little push in the right direction, so he fought your battle for you."

Charlotte grabs my cell phone off of my nightstand and thrusts it towards me. "Now, be a good girl, call him and tell him thank you and that you owe him an unlimited amount of blow jobs."

I start to reach for the phone but then drop my hand. While I am absolutely grateful that he did something like this for me, that still doesn't solve our other problem.

"Charlotte, I don't know. I mean, I can handle a lot of things. I HAVE handled a lot of things, but the My Little Pony thing might be pushing it. He may have saved my ass with mom, but that still doesn't change the fact that this fetish or whatever you want to call it is just plain weird. There's a thing called BronyCon, Charlotte. BRONYCON. I might have to dress up as a horse and go to this thing every year for the rest of my life. I don't know if I'm ready for that," I admit.

Charlotte pushes herself up from my bed and grabs her bag that she dropped by my door. "I figured you would say something like that, so I brought something that might help."

She digs inside and pulls out a wrapped present, holding it up for me to see.

"You bought me another Christmas present?"

Charlotte rolls her eyes and tosses it to me. "No, that is the present from Tyler you never opened."

I blink back tears and stare down at the gift, afraid to open it. In all the commotion on Christmas, I totally forgot that he got me something. I shoved it under the tree to open later on and, after our fight, I didn't want anything to do with it.

"Well, open it!"

With a sniffle, I rip into the paper and stare in confusion at what I'm holding in my hand.

"Bronies: A Documentary," I read aloud. "Seriously?"

Charlotte pulls a folded piece of paper out of her purse and hands it to me. "This came with it too. Sorry, I already read it."

Snatching the paper out of her hand, I give her a dirty look before unfolding it and quickly reading through Tyler's hand-written note.

Dear Ava,

I know this isn't as awesome as another pair of fancy shoes, but I hope it will help explain things a little better. I want you to know everything about me - the good, the bad and the just plain fucking weird. I hope after you watch this, you'll understand me and where I'm coming from. I want to tell you that I adore you, but Gavin is looking over my shoulder and he told me that's too gay. So, I'll just end this note by telling you that you amaze me and I'm so glad you let me see you naked.

Love,
Tyler

"Look, I didn't get this whole thing either, but after I read that note, Gavin sat me down and explained everything to me and then made me watch Tyler's copy of that DVD. If I have to suffer through this documentary to try and understand a guy I'm NOT in love with, then it's only fair you do the same since you ARE in love with him."

Setting the note aside, I stare down at the DVD. "Charlotte, he thinks he can find his real dad at BronyCon. I want to support him, but that's just too crazy even for me."

She sighs and perches on the edge of my bed. "Ava, I think deep down he knows he's not truly going to find his real dad there. You need to understand how important this is to him. You need to realize how much he just wants to know and understand where he came from. It's a pipe dream that he'll find his dad out of all of those people, but it gives him hope. No one has ever understood the whole Brony thing he's got going on, aside from other Bronies. He just wants his real dad to be someone who understands him."

Sixty minutes after Charlotte left, I'm sitting on the floor in my room crying harder than I've ever cried in my life. Friendship IS magic. Tyler is part of a community that believes in friendship and being happy, why is that so bad? People only think it's weird because they don't understand it, but these horses are role models! Fluttershy represents people with crippling social anxieties and Twilight Sparkle embodies bookish people without making them look like nerds. It's genius!

It's about people trying to belong! Sure, they dress up like ponies and there's Cloppers and Furries and other things I don't understand, but that's not the point. These people don't want to have sex with ponies or do weird shit with them. Okay, some do, but not the majority. Most of them are simply looking for friendship and a place where they belong, a concept I'm very familiar with. All this time I've been looking for a place to belong.

My mom tried to make it be Seduction and Snacks and I was miserable. Fashion is where I belong, and talking to other people about fashion. Tyler found his place to belong a long time ago and who am I to discourage that?

I immediately get out of bed and fire up my laptop. Hopefully I'm not too late and I can still do this. I'm going to show Tyler once and for all that I'm not afraid. He fought my battle for me with my mom, but I'm going to fight this one for him. I'm going to make sure everyone understands what I love about him.

As soon as I get what I need printed off of my laptop, I head towards my door just as my mom comes through it.

We stand there staring at each other awkwardly for a few minutes before she finally speaks. "I don't like apologizing."

I nod. "Me either."

Glad we established that.

"I forgive you for not wanting to work at Seduction and Snacks."

"And I forgive you for not understanding my dream," I tell her.

She leans in and wraps her arms around me. I slide my arms around her shoulders and hug her back.

"You're totally my favorite child," she whispers before pulling back.

"You just said that same thing to Charlotte a few minutes ago, didn't you?"

She shrugs. "Does it matter?"

"Nope."

I thrust my arm out and hand her one of the print-outs. "Now that we like each other again and Tyler made you cry, I expect you to be there."

She looks over the page and then gives me a questioning look. "You have got to be kidding me."

"I would never kid about something like this."

Mom looks back down at the paper. "If I go to this, can I make fun of people?"

I start to tell her no and then think better of it. If I tell her no, she definitely won't come and I need her to be there. "You can only make fun of people if they make fun of you first."

She thinks about this for a few seconds before nodding. "I can deal with that."

I walk out of my bedroom with a smile on my face, making plans in my head and hoping that everything works.

CHAPTER 28

BronyCon

- Tyler -

"I still don't understand why I have to be blindfolded. Are you going to do some weird, kinky shit to me?"

Gavin laughs and I feel his car come to a stop as he turns off the engine.

"Sorry, no kinky shit for you today, my friend. Today, your dreams are coming true," Gavin tells me.

I hear him open his car door and get out and, a few seconds later, he's opening my door and helping me out of the car.

"My dreams already came true. Liz finally showed me the masturbation room," I tell him as he slams my door closed and starts leading me away.

"I still can't believe she did that. Aunt Liz didn't even tell *me* about that room until a month ago," Gavin complains.

We walk in silence for a few minutes and I'm about ready to bitch at him again for the blindfold when I hear him speak to someone and a rustling of papers.

"Two adults? Very good. Have a magical day!"

Gavin thanks the guy and continues pulling me forward. We walk through a door and I'm suddenly assaulted with the sounds of hundreds of laughing people, a bunch of them bumping into me as we make our way through a crowd.

"Okay, I think it's safe to remove the blindfold now," Gavin announces.

I feel his hands at the back of my head and I'm blinking at the bright lights and colors that surround me a few seconds later.

This can't be happening. There is no fucking way this is real.

"Am I dreaming?" I whisper as a guy in a Twilight Sparkle costume walks by me and smiles.

There's My Little Ponies as far as the eye can see. MLP costumes, MLP toys, stuffed animals, games, signs and face painting. There are televisions lining the walls playing episodes of MLP, there are people acting out scenes on one side of me and voice actors from the show signing autographs on another. It's so beautiful I want to cry.

"Oh, fuck, it's Tara Strong, the voice of Twilight Sparkle," I say excitedly, pointing over to one table. "Shit, that's Peter New, the voice of Macintosh! Peter New is here, Peter New is here!"

I start jumping up and down, clapping my hands together like a fool, but I don't care! I'm at BronyCon, motherfuckers!

Gavin laughs, grabbing my arm to turn me around. When I see what's behind me, I really do start to get choked up. Standing in a group is everyone I love and none of them look the least bit uncomfortable surrounded by My Little Ponies.

My mom and dad are the first ones to approach me, both of them wrapping their arms around me.

"We just wanted to tell you that we love you and we accept you just the way you are," my mom tells me. "I've already been asked to speak on a panel about the negative implications regarding Bronies and perversion. Isn't that exciting?"

My dad pats me on the back and smiles. "Even though you're not my son by blood, you're the son of my heart and that's all that matters. Also, your mother now wants to try out one of those Brony butt plugs later on tonight, so thanks for that."

I cringe and back away from him as Liz and Claire both come up to me.

"We'd both like to thank you for your love of all things Brony because after being here for fifteen minutes, we've already been asked by BronyCon if they could be an official sponsor for Seduction and Snacks," Liz tells me.

Claire nods. "I was even asked to make a thousand pony-shaped cookies for next year's event."

Carter and Jim walk up to me next and my eyes widen in surprise when I see that they're both wearing MLP t-shirts.

"Oh, my gosh, are you guys going to be Bronies now? Do you want to come to my next meeting?" I ask them excitedly.

Jim holds up his hand. "Whoa, slow your roll. This shit is still weird as fuck, but I will admit that I like the way this shirt looks on me."

Carter shrugs, looking down at his own shirt that says 'BRONY' in big, black letters across the chest with a picture of Applejack under it. "I don't know, man, everyone here is so friendly. The guys at the face-painting booth told me I had nice bone structure. I could hang with them."

Even though I'm in the best place ever and all of these people have come to support me, there's still someone missing. Before I have a chance to dwell on it, I hear a throat clear behind me. I turn around and my jaw drops.

Ava stands there with her hands on her hips wearing a tight, pink bustier, a pink tutu and white, knee-high boots. She does a slow turn and attached to the ass of her skirt is a multi-colored tail that hangs down to her knees. She looks over her shoulder at me and shakes her ass and it takes everything in me not to throw her to the ground and climb her like a fucking pine tree.

I walk over to her as she completes her turn. She slides her hands up my chest and around my shoulders, clasping them together at the back of my neck.

"You are the hottest fucking woman I have ever seen in my life," I tell her softly as she smiles up at me.

"I hope this makes up for the fact that I was a total bitch to you. I should have never said the things I did."

I shake my head at her. "No, I was an asshole. I pushed you too far and I said some really shitty things when all I wanted to do was tell you that I love you."

Ava closes her eyes and sighs, pressing her lips to mine. She feels so right and so amazing in my arms that I let out a groan of disappointment when she moves away.

"I kind of like this look on me and I'm having a great time here. I think I'm going to like being in love with a Brony," she admits.

"Is this your way of telling me that you were completely wrong about Bronies and they aren't weird at all?" I ask with a laugh.

She thinks about it for a minute and then smiles. "I don't like apologizing, but when I'm wrong, I say I'm wrong."

I smile right back at her. "You looked wonderful out there. Nobody puts Ava in a corner."

We hear a groan and turn to see Drew and Jenny standing arm-in-arm.

"Did you two vaginas just quote *Dirty Dancing*?" Drew asks.

"Drew? What the fuck are you doing here?" Carter asks. "I thought you said you had a meeting today and couldn't get together with us."

"And what the mother of fucks are you wearing?" Jim questions, looking him up and down.

"You didn't tell me you guys were coming to BronyCon, you just said you were doing something to surprise Tyler," Drew explains. "And I'll have you know, this pony costume is one-hundred-percent fleece and the tail is made from genuine unicorn hair."

We all stare at Drew's pink, plush horse costume, complete with a giant stuffed horse head that he's currently carrying under his arm.

"My balls are sweating like a motherfucker in this thing, but it's totally worth it," he tells us with a smile.

"And the best part is, Drew hasn't been cheating on me!" Jenny announces with glee.

Drew sighs and takes a step forward. "I can't live with the shame and the guilt anymore, guys. I'm tired of lying by omission and not living my life the way I was meant to live it. Everyone, today I am officially coming out as a Brony."

A few passers-by stop when they hear Drew's announcement and start clapping and cheering for him.

"Shit! That's where I recognized the glitter from on your hand that day at work," I say suddenly. "That's the glitter we use at Brony meetings when we do the handshake. You've been secretly going to Brony meetings!"

Gavin leans in closer to me. "Dude, I thought you said there wasn't a handshake?"

I scoff at him. "Like I was going to admit all the Brony secrets to you. It's against the code, man."

My mom lets go of my dad's hand and walks up to Drew, staring at him for a few minutes. Drew stares right back, squinting like he's trying to get a better look at her.

"Don't I know you from somewhere?" Drew finally asks.

My mom nods. "You look familiar too, but I just can't place it."

I look back and forth between them, wondering what the hell is going on.

"Have you ever worked at the strip club Jennie's Juggs?" Drew asks.

My mom shakes her head. "Nope."

Drew brings one of his horse hoof hands up to his face and scratches his cheek. "What about Starbutts? They used to have this great show with two chicks and a couple of ping-pong balls. You sort of look like one of them."

My mom shakes her head again.

Drew eyes suddenly go wide and he lifts his hoof up in the air. "I REMEMBER! Aren't you the chick I had that foursome with in college? You're name's Debbie or Dinda or something, right?"

"Oh, my God," Gavin mutters next to me.

I'm still trying to figure out what the fuck is going on right now when I feel Ava squeeze my hand.

"Donna, my name is Donna," my mom tells him with a smile.

"That's it! Donna! Well, shit, it's good to see you again," he tells her before turning to Carter. "Dude, this was the chick I banged the night you met Claire, remember?"

"I thought you passed out in the bathtub the night we met?" Claire asks.

Drew and my mom laugh and the sound makes a little bit of vomit come up in my throat.

"I totally passed out in the tub, but that was after the foursome. Actually, now that I think about it, weren't you in the tub with me?" Drew asks my mom.

She laughs again and nods. "I was. I woke up the next morning curled up in that thing alone wondering what the hell had happened."

"Oh, holy fuck," Ava whispers.

No. No, no, no. This is not happening. This is NOT fucking happening!

Drew shakes his head in regret. "Damn. I didn't even realize I left you in there. I got up to take a piss and couldn't stop laughing about the fact that I still had the condom on, stuck to my penis."

I let out the breath I've been holding and send a prayer up to heaven.

"Too bad that fucker was totally broke and hanging in pieces around my junk," Drew continues. "Good thing nothing bad ever came from that, huh?"

Drew and my mom keep right on laughing, not even realizing that everyone is staring at them and I'm about ready to lose my shit all over this place.

Claire steps forward and looks back and forth between Drew and I. Her eyes widen and she does it again. Back and forth and back and forth until I want to run screaming out of this place.

"Oh, sweet Christ," she finally mutters.

My mom finally stops laughing and mimics Claire, looking between Drew and me.

"Oh. Oh, my," she whispers.

Drew puts his hoof hands on his hips and glares at the two of them.

"Well, you wanted to come to BronyCon and find your dad," Ava tells me. "Congratulations, sweetie."

I bend at the waist and rest my hands on my knees, taking in as many deep breaths as I can without passing out.

Drew huffs. "What? I don't get it."

ePILOGUe

~ Ava ~

Three months later...

"Are you sure you're using enough lube? I don't think you're using enough."

"Shut up, I totally know what I'm doing, I watched a couple of Youtube videos."

"You're not going to tell anyone about this, right? I mean, this is awesome and everything and I love you and trust you, but I don't need this shit getting out."

"Will you stop complaining? Do you want to do this or not?" I demand.

Holding the MLP butt plug up in the air, I glare at Tyler. He's clutching onto the table in the masturbation room at Seduction and Snacks, sticking his bare ass out, looking at me over his shoulder.

"Stop yelling at me! I can't relax if you keep yelling at me," he complains.

In hindsight, sneaking off to the masturbation room in the middle of Charlotte and Gavin's co-ed bridal shower probably wasn't the best idea, but we got bored watching them open up all of those stupid pots and pans and monogrammed towels.

Running my hand down Tyler's back, I lean in closer to him and whisper in his ear. "Calm down, baby, I totally know what I'm doing."

He sighs and turns his face, pressing his lips to mine. I glide my tongue across his bottom lip before pushing it between his lips. His tongue tangles with mine and I feel a gentle tug as he sucks it into his mouth. As the kiss continues, I can feel Tyler relaxing and I know he's getting excited.

"JESUS FUCKING CHRIST!" he suddenly screams, breaking the kiss and jumping away from the table.

"Sorry! Sorry, oh hell, I got a little carried away. I didn't mean to stick it all the way in!" I apologize, wincing at him as he gives me a dirty look.

He tries to twist and turn his body to look at his ass and when he does, the tail attached to the butt plug swishes back and forth across the back of his legs. I can't help it, I smack my hand over my mouth and start laughing.

"THIS IS NOT FUNNY! THIS IS NOT FUCKING FUNNY!" he yells, trying to grab for the tail to pull the entire thing out but it keeps swishing away from his reach. "GET THIS DAMN THING OUT OF MY ASS!"

I really wasn't sure I would ever be able to handle the weird shit Tyler likes to do in the bedroom but right now, I realize all of my fears were for nothing. Tyler's very good about throwing some normal, but equally hot sex into the mix every once in a while and I'm a strong, independent woman who can handle anything life throws at me. Including a hot guy dancing around a dark room trying to yank a horse tail out of his ass.

My website is still doing amazing and my mom even sponsored an ad on it for Seduction and Snacks. She's still a little sad that I won't be spending the rest of my life working in the family business, but she's accepted the fact that this is what I want to do and she's happy for me.

"Will you hold still? I can't get it out if you're going to keep flailing all over the place," I scold Tyler, walking over to him and grabbing his arms.

"I promise I will never, ever ask you for anal again. This is serious business right here and not for amateurs. I don't think I'll ever be able to take a proper shit again," he complains.

Standing up on my tiptoes, I kiss his lips and smile at him. "I love you, but you're a lying sack of shit. You know you're going to ask me tomorrow if it's Anal Friday yet."

"One of these days, it really will be Anal Friday and you'll be glad I asked," he tells me, turning around so I can get to his ass.

"You know, this tail really is quite pretty. I think you should leave it in for a while. I could brush it and maybe put a braid in it."

Tyler growls at me over his shoulder. "You made your point. From now on, I will think twice before calling you a wuss for not trying out a new toy."

I kiss the back of his shoulder and move to yank on the tail when the door to the room bursts open and Drew walks in.

"Come on, kid, it's time for us to play catch!"

After BronyCon, Drew and Tyler had a DNA test done and the results were fairly conclusive. Drew is now the proud father of another bouncing baby boy. Ever since the test results came back, he's been overcompensating the father thing just a little bit.

Tyler and I freeze and Drew crosses his arms in front of him, tapping his toe in irritation. "Son, I am really disappointed in you right now."

Tyler quickly reaches down around his ankles for his pants and pulls them up, the tail refusing to be hidden and, instead, drapes outside of his pants.

"It's not what it looks like," Tyler tries to explain, swatting at the tail to try and keep it out of sight.

Drew shakes his head at Tyler. "How many times do I have to tell you? When you're trying new, kinky shit, always get that stuff on camera. It's like you were raised in a barn or something."

Drew turns and walks back out of the room, throwing a parting comment over his shoulder. "Shake a tail feather, dick bag, I still need to teach you how to ride a bike!"

The door slams closed behind him and I slide my arms around Gavin's waist and look up at him. "Uncle Drew is aware that you already know how to ride a bike, right?"

Tyler pulls me in closer. "Who the fuck knows? Yesterday, he gave me the 'birds and the bees' talk and it included props and scenes he acted out with your Aunt Jenny. I can never look her in the eyes ever again."

I laugh, grabbing onto Tyler's face and pulling him down for a kiss. I'm pretty sure no one has a crazier life than I do, but that's okay. My closet is filled with couture and My Little Pony costumes, I have a job I'm ecstatic about, I'm in love with a crazy guy and my sister is getting married. It really doesn't get any better than this - or any stranger.

The door to the room opens up again and all we see is a very large, very creepy looking fist stick through the crack.

"Duke says get your horse's ass out here. It's time for cake!"

The fist disappears and the door quickly slams closed.

I look up at Tyler in confusion and he shakes his head at me.

"Don't ask."

I take that back. The strange just never ends.

♘ THE END ♘

If you or anyone you know might be
struggling with an addiction to My Little Pony, you're not alone.
Be proud, be loud and share the magic.
http://bronycon.org/

ACKNOWLEDGEMENTS

First and foremost, thank you to Janet Burns for being the best assistant a girl could ever ask for. Your love and support means the world to me and I'm so thankful to have you in my life.

Thank you to C.C. Wood for being the light in my life and my inspiration. You are my hero, and the wind beneath my wings.

To Beth Ehemann for telling me I don't suck and for being a wonderful friend. I'm so glad I met you and found out we were separated at birth, as well as our husbands.

To Stephanie Johnson for being an amazing human being, a great friend and the best cookie whore in the entire world.

Thank you to Robin Stranahan for being the best assistant in NOLA and for all the MLP gifts, especially the Brony documentary. I love your face!

Special thanks to the women from Pure Romance of Cincinnati for giving me a tour of the warehouse, and inspiration for this book...especially turkey giblets.

Thank you to Valerie Potjeau, Christie Silva, Tressa Sager and

Jamie Sager Hall for bringing dolphin rape awareness into the public light.

To Rapey the Dolphin for providing the answers to all of life's questions.

Thank you to the fans all over the world for embracing the craziness of these characters and for allowing me to release the insanity in my brain to the pages of a book.

Thank you to my nephew for not being afraid to be a Brony and for letting me poke just a little bit of fun at you.

Thank you to Donna and Nikki for your amazing support and for not running away in fear when you read my manuscripts. And my texts. And my emails. Mostly my texts.

Last but not least, to my poor family who have five-minute conversations with me before I even realize they've been talking. Thank you for loving me even when I forget your names and I start taking notes about stories in the middle of dinner.

2071

Made in the USA
San Bernardino, CA
13 March 2014